Ravings of an Unsettled Mind

Written and collected by J.A. Barrios

Also by J.A. Barrios:

Tenebris: The Unholy Darkness

Art Credits
Cover illustration: Jaeger Spratt
Graphic design: Luis Gallardo
Interior pencils: J.A. Barrios
Interior inks: Jaeger Spratt
Photography: Marcus Rousey

This is a work of Fiction. Names, characters, and incidents are products of the author's imagination and are not to be construed as real. Any resemblance to actual events, locales, organizations, or persons, living or dead, are coincidental or fictionalized.

for Jennifer,

Ravings of an
Unsettled Mind

Enjoy these tales of
TERROR!

Dedication

I dedicate this to Geoffrey Bardos, especially the story "Inheritance." Of all people, I wish you had the chance to read that one. I will miss you, brother.

I also wish to dedicate this to mental health, to those struggling through grief and depression. To the addicts, those both in and out of recovery. To the ones who feel like there is nothing left but the ultimate choice – I want you to know that you are not alone, and I will always fight for you.

"We have such sights to show you."

-Pinhead, *Hellraiser*

(Clive Barker)

Table of Contents

Author's Introduction

As a child I feared everything: the dark, monsters, and all bugs (yes, even ladybugs). The most shameful were Yoda and E.T. the extraterrestrial. What a chump, right? It kept me from enjoying things like playing outdoors and sleeping without a lamp on, or even by myself (thanks for putting up with me, Daniel).

I used to have nightmares all the time, especially a recurring one involving E.T. himself. Mainly because I couldn't stop watching that movie despite having to close my eyes every time the titular character was on screen.

Of course, these sensitivities weren't all created equally. I loved Godzilla, and none of the monsters he fought ever gave me nightmares. Yoda scared me, but *Gremlins* was fine. I loved watching *Goosebumps*, although I did have to cover my eyes during the intro whenever that dog's eyes glowed... which didn't stop my brother from pausing the tapes right at the dog part – thanks a lot!

I don't remember the age, but it must have been around the first or second grade when I saw Stephen King's *Creepshow* for the first time. I fell in love. *Pet Sematary*, *Cat's Eye*, and *IT* were all movies I grew to love, and it even gave me the ambition to start writing scary stories. But, yes, I was still plagued by nightmares!

Eventually, only two recurring nightmares still haunted me: my best friend, Brian, pulling off his face and chasing me

1

around making E.T. noises, and being asleep in the back of the car while my dad and oldest brother, Carlos, drove me to the top of a very high mountain then got out and pushed the car down with me still inside. Over time I found ways to take action and conquer those dreams. The nightmares were over.

Finally, peace at last! By middle school I no longer had stupid nightmares and didn't jump every time I saw E.T. or Yoda. However, I began to feel like something was missing. What could a child with lots of toys and a loving family possibly need? It was the fear. The very thing that tormented me for so long became something of longing. I remember the very last movie to give me a nightmare was John Carpenter's *In the Mouth of Madness*. I watched it again – nothing. I started watching all the horror movies in our large VHS tape collection which filled a closet. Still no nightmares.

It then became an obsession with the spooky, the macabre; these were things I needed in my life. Horror became my favorite movie genre. I took that early ambition to write scary stories and started doing exactly that. Now, these stories I present to you here are not those same childhood stories. One was basically a rip-off of *Night of the Creeps*, so I can't use that. Another involves Greek mythology, but that's on the back burner for something more full-length.

Over the last several years, inspired by Inktober, I tried to write a different short story every week of October. Some of those are here. Others are inspired by dreams I've had. And some are just a peek into what I carry with me everywhere I go. I hope you enjoy, and maybe even find some horror thrills yourself!

Acceptance

My brother and I were on a scenic drive to go camping. I no longer recall the time of year. It was so very long ago, and temperature is not something I have much grasp of anymore. Images, however, I still retain. It was green, I remember that. The grass-covered valleys we drove through, winding roads snaking between cow pastures, were a vivid green. Between the fields, hillsides were thick with lush, beautiful trees. The sky was a clear blue, the sun shining down on all the green. We were ready for a good time.

I remember having several siblings but this was my closest. My favorite. We did almost everything together, caused trouble together. I was something of an oddball, a black sheep, but so was he. It was always the two of us, so there was never a time I felt out of place. We had each other and the vast wilderness at our fingertips.

We drove past fields and valleys, then there were sloping green mountains we passed as we approached closer to the mountain that was our destination. The sun was moving. The clouds were forming. Our mountain, our fate, began to loom large on the horizon.

I honestly could not say how we got to that road. Life takes you down many roads. This is true, but I don't know at which point it took us there. Again, it has been so long I only recall being on the road and the knowledge of our destination drawing us forward.

The skies became orange as we climbed the narrow roads up our mountain. It was fortunate we were almost there, for darkness was about to fall and we needed to be settled in by then. The drive up to the summit was not as quick as we travelers would have hoped. We curved around and around the mountain, watching the purpling of the sky and trying not to look over the side of the road to where there was no more pavement, only a sheer drop.

We reached a plateau and saw the tall, silver gate in the fence surrounding the campgrounds. We stopped just before the gate and looked to the little kiosk on the side. The car sat idling for a moment until we realized nobody was there. We continued forward. Fortunate, we thought, that the gate was open.

Once on the compound we could see the quaint wooden cabins. We passed a small parking lot for day hikers to hit the trails. The road continued further up to the rest of the cabins and we were still not at our destination yet, not quite.

It was now dark, but not in the way it should be at night. The light had more of a grayish hue, as if the sun were still high, only obscured by thick clouds. I couldn't see clearly though, or so I thought. All the trees visible around the compound seemed to be stripped of their leaves, twisted in wicked ways, but I chalked it up to the strange darkness that wasn't so dark.

"Stop!" My brother shouted and I slammed my foot onto the break.

We came to a screeching halt. The engine purred ever so gently, and we both stared at the cabin to our right. This was not my cabin, but my brother insisted he go down. That he *must.* I argued with him that our destination was still further ahead, but he was certain that this was *his* cabin. As if we got separate cabins!

I let him out of the car, figuring I would go to where we were supposed to be and he'd soon see he was mistaken and come find me later. The compound wasn't terribly large so he shouldn't have any trouble finding me. There was just one road and two directions, forwards or back.

I began to drive up an incline with two more cabins on either side of the road. The steep road curved to the left, and there ahead of me was the final cabin on the compound. My cabin. I parked my car by it, and as I stepped out a distinct scent caught my nose. It was foul, almost like rotten eggs. It made me dizzy and I felt as if I were in a fog. I certainly had to get indoors now.

I did not take any bags in my hands. I'm not sure there were ever any bags to begin with, as I think of it now. I approached my cabin. The door swung open towards me, revealing an imposing dark figure in the doorway. It was frightening, but not as frightening as the blaze of flames I could see within the cabin. I stood there frozen as the person stepped out, revealing itself not to be a person at all.

I had never beheld such a gruesome appearance. The being was bulbous, though still humanoid, with straps of dried skin bound around parts of its body. Rolls of its pale veiny flesh bulged out around the tanned leather strapped across its form. Barbed wire wrapped around its two arms and twisted across its eyes and nose as well. Streaks of blood dripped down its fat cheeks where the barbs pierced its flesh.

I did the only sensible thing to do: I screamed and ran away.

I ran back to the road and down the hill, heading for the cabins at the bottom. The beast did not rush after me. It was slow and took its steps with ease. It hardly seemed to be chasing me at all, but I still couldn't shake the feeling that it was.

I made it inside one of the cabins. To my shock the interior of this cabin was crowded with stacks of cash and a single man inside. I screamed at the man for help, but he seemed not to notice me at all. He kept at the task before him, attempting to stash his money in a small box. It seemed impossible all that money could ever fit into one little container, but he was determined in his frenzy. That wasn't my concern though. The creature in my cabin was all I could think of.

I continued to yell for help as I grabbed the man to shake him. Once I had grasped him though, I found I was utterly unable to move him. That's when I saw it. Another one of those beings.

This one was not hulking and round like the one at my cabin, but slim and lanky. It watched the man, its crooked body bound in leathery straps. Now its horrible gaze shifted to me. Unlike the fat one, this beast's barbed wire wrapped around its head covering the mouth, piercing into its lips. At some point in time, it must have had a nose, but the dully scarred flesh around the nose hole suggested that was long, long ago. The eyes, though! They were exposed alright, the skin of the being's eyelids had been peeled away entirely which made its raw, red-ringed stare all the more penetrating.

Acceptance

I stumbled back and rushed out the door. The obese figure now stood outside the door waiting for me, grunting. I turned and ran behind the cabin. I went straight for the fence surrounding the campground. I don't know what I was thinking, the fence was too high to consider climbing and there was nothing on the other side but trees. I shook the fence and screamed anyway, futilely calling for help and staring through at the trees on the other side.

It was then I finally saw clearly that these were no ordinary trees. They had lost all their leaves and the naked branches twisted unnaturally, like gnarled witches' fingers scratching at the sky. They swayed back and forth with the coming wind and howled like the most tortured souls to ever exist. Yes, that's right, the trees howled, and from their agony I saw the faces. These were not mere oaks, but some god-forsaken abomination of trees and humans. Long distorted faces were embedded into the bark of each tree, and that sound they made…

I was so disturbed I didn't hear the *thing* approach until it snapped a twig. At the sound, the icy weight of panic dropped into my gut and jolted me into action. I ran past my pursuer to the cabin across the road. I went in with ease and hurriedly shut the door behind me as the being merely turned its head in my direction, slowly watching my panicked retreat.

Leaning against the closed door to catch my breath for a moment, I took in this cabin's interior. It was completely quiet and dark, but the faint light coming through the windows gave the room a reddish hue.

Above me I could make out the dim shape of a balcony overlooking this front room. My eyes adjusted, I quickly found the staircase to reach it. Along the wall as I went up the stairs there were several paintings. First was a large plantation-style house with a wealthy White family standing in front of it while their dark-skinned servants worked in the yard. The next painting was a portrait of a White male in a Confederate soldier's gray uniform. The last was another family portrait, this time missing the man.

As I reached the top of the steps, I heard a loud crash from one of the upstairs rooms. I set my eyes on the door, unsure whether to investigate it or leave it be. I looked down to the front door of the cabin and thought of that grotesque thing after me. It had yet to come in, but perhaps I should find something or someone that could help.

There was another sound coming from the closed room, I could hear a person inside. It was a man who sounded distressed. I opened the door to find a blonde-haired man who in the process of tearing the room apart. By the dim light outside, I could see the bed was flipped over, a dresser turned onto its side, and clothing was scattered throughout. Opening the door had startled him and he turned to me with a plank of wood gripped firmly in his hands.

"They everywhere, boy!" the man said with a crazed panic in his eyes. "They gon' get me!"

"There's one after me too!" I couldn't hide my fear, "I don't know what to—"

"LOOK OUT!" the man shouted and swung the wood. I jumped out of the way as he slammed it onto the floor. I was staring at the part of the floor he had smashed, but then I saw the man's gaze was fixed on the corner behind the door.

"I got you now," he said, a merciless grin spreading across his face.

I pulled the door back to get a look at who the man was talking to. I was puzzled to see there was just an old ragged, homemade-looking doll. My stomach nearly lept up into my throat when I saw that it jumped, startled, when it saw me. The doll was alive!

Before I could even process what I had seen, the disturbing thing moved faster than my eyes could follow and had jumped onto the man. He stumbled back and then, seemingly out of nowhere, a swarm of dolls leapt out of the gloom, clinging onto him. He screamed and thrashed as the hoard of dolls attacked him, their malicious giggles filling the small room.

I rushed out of the room when two of the dolls began looking at me. They pursued, and several more of the creepy little dolls joined in the chase as I retreated. After a few steps though, I realized I had no place to run to.

I stopped short at the balcony I spotted from the entrance and gripped the railing. Leaning over it to look, I saw with yet another nasty shock the *creature* was there. The fat man, the *thing*, whatever it was, stood in the center of the floor, the door wide open behind it, looking up at me. I don't know how it could see through the barbed wire across its eyes, but I could feel its gaze directly on me.

I was trapped. The dolls approached with menacing laughter and the only escape was over the balcony. It was only now that I thought of my brother. I should have run to where I'd left him, hoping he wasn't being pursued by one of these things as well. The being standing there in the living room slowly raised up a hand, as if offering for me come down, to take it. I had a choice, the dolls or this...

I braced myself against the railing and jumped over, crashing to the ground. I screamed as if in agony, but to be truthful, I do not believe I even had a moment of pain. It was all in my mind. The corpulent creature stood above me, hand extended, and I took its grasp.

The creature held me tight in its clutches as we walked back to my cabin, slowly. A burning stench was growing stronger. I tried struggling out of its grip but could not break free. As we approached my cabin, I could see the flames through the windows within. Then the creature spoke.

"If you accept the fear, you will be in the clear." The being's voice was soft, almost kind. It ripped away my clothes in one simple, swift motion.

"No, no! The fire!" I screamed. "Don't put me in the fire!"

Seemingly from nowhere a garment of leathery flesh appeared in the creature's hand. It spoke again, "If you fight it, you will burn." It paused and wrapped the flesh tight around my waist, then finished with, "If you accept it, you will learn."

The being gestured to the door.

I took in a deep, sulfuric breath as the door slowly opened to me again. Flames stung at the doorway of my destination. Those words repeated in my head, "If you fight it you will burn; if you accept it, you will learn."

I looked back at my guide once more and it handed me a domed helmet. I took a peep inside. Within the helmet were dozens of tiny razor-sharp needles. I placed the helmet onto my head. The needles pierced my flesh. I felt the rivulets of blood running down my neck as I stepped into the cool welcoming blanket of flames.

I was home.

Stalker

Thump, thump, thump.

Old Thomas Gregory nailed yet another wooden plank across the back door. He was nearly done boarding it up. The front door to his cabin had already been sealed shut. More planks, bedposts, broken chairs, and the ruins of a table were scattered in piles around the corners of the main room.

Thomas had been busy for hours, and for days before that. He had arrived at the family cabin three days ago and got to work immediately. He began by destroying the tables and chairs and any other wooden furniture he could find, using the old axe from the shed. After much struggle to push the heavy sofa-bed to block the front door, Thomas had dragged a couple of mattresses down the stairs to add to his blockade. He couldn't remember when he had slept last.

Finally, three days later, most of the windows were sealed off, just two remained untouched. His eyes were ablaze, bloodshot from tiredness, desperate to finish the final plank on the back door. He was exhausted. The speed of his movement had suffered tremendously as each day went on.

A single oil lamp sat on the kitchen floor. The dim orange light was sufficient to see the open box of rusted nails near his foot as it cast his enlarged shadow flickering on the wall behind him. So close to completion, Thomas found renewed strength and his hammering picked up speed.

Thump, thump, thump.

He hammered the final nail in and turned to his next target, a window across from him, through the doorway. Thomas left the lamp in the kitchen and walked into the living room, passing the blazing fireplace. The dancing flames illuminated the room as he approached, hammer and box of nails in hands.

Thomas looked through the frost-crusted glass. It was dark and quiet outside. The snowfall was heavy and hadn't stopped for the past week. It had been hell getting to the cabin through this weather, but Thomas was determined.

Thump, thump, thump.

He began to nail a plank in the right corner. The chill air seeped through the window even as the heat from the fireplace warmed his back. He hammered down the left side of the plank.

Thump, thump–

Thomas paused, hammer in midair, then moved his face closer to the window.

The falling snow swirled madly in the harsh winds. It was nearly impossible for Thomas to see further than a few feet out the window. He held his breath to keep it from fogging the glass. A short distance away, there IT was. He gasped and stepped back, startled. The dark humanoid silhouette.

"It's here!" Thomas gasped.

He continued to stare as the figure stood in the snow, perfectly still. Thomas held his breath. Fear spiked inside his head. He had been expecting this moment, when the figure would find him again. Now as he watched IT, Thomas still couldn't believe the moment had come.

Time slipped past, staring at the still figure. Suddenly IT stirred and started moving forward. Quickly, Thomas darted for more wood. His hammer banged away with renewed urgency. His arms stung and his feet were sore. Finishing on another side, he peeked out the window again. The black figure was closer. The wind didn't seem to hinder ITs slow but persistent stalk. Thomas boarded up another part, then another, finally covering most of the glass.

"You ain't gettin' in here!" Thomas shouted and swept to the last window. He quickly peered out, then, satisfied nothing was there, turned to grab another plank. Right as Thomas placed the wood over the window– *CRASH*! The form of an arm, blacker than black, the pure absence of light, broke through a pane of glass and snatched at Thomas.

"No! Get back! Get back!" Thomas croaked, swinging his hammer. He pelted the mysterious hand twice before it retracted, disappearing into the blizzard.

Thomas worked his hammer fiercely, boarding up the final window as the frigid air flowed in. His heart raced with panic. Once the final nails had been secured, Thomas let out one long sigh of relief and went to sit by the fire.

There was a harsh bang at the door, but Thomas paid no mind. He laughed, actually. The kind of crazed laughter only the demented could make, recognizable to those walking the halls of a mental asylum. His laughing grew more hysterical, twisting into a sob.

Thomas thought of his family. How long ago it seemed now, when he had a normal life. Before IT came for him. Thomas' sobs wracked his elderly frame as he recalled his granddaughter, age four, playing in the garden when the figure had first appeared.

The strange black figure, a silhouette from every angle even in bright daylight, had seemingly appeared from nowhere. IT grabbed her, holding her up by the hair as she squealed for her mommy. Francis, Thomas' son-in-law, had rushed out gripping a bat with both hands, a foolish knight coming to the rescue. Thomas stayed inside, holding onto his daughter, Mary, as they watched from the kitchen window.

Francis swung once, only once, before the silhouetted figure snatched the bat from his grasp. IT dropped the child and bat onto the grass, then lunged at Francis, gouging out his eyes. The girl let out a long shrill scream at the blood and fluid streaking down her father's cheeks.

"Oh god! Oh no!" Mary rushed out. No weapon, no plan, just the need to get to her little girl.

Thomas stood frozen by the doorway. Not even his daughter pushing him to the side had snapped him out of it. He couldn't believe his eyes. His son-in-law crumpled on the ground. His daughter and granddaughter held each other tight. The thing grabbed them and tore them apart.

A few weeks before this happened, Thomas had left his house to live with his daughter. He couldn't shake the feeling he was being watched, as if something was coming for him. Thomas first started feeling this way six months before, shortly after his wife Nora had passed.

Stalker

They'd lived happily together for 42 years, had a son, Avery, who stayed busy traveling for work and a daughter who still lived in town. His wife loved birdwatching, and every winter Thomas would keep busy in his workshop building birdhouses for her to put out in their garden in the spring.

Nora had gotten cancer a few years before and beat it, fully in remission. At least, that's what they thought. Then one day, they'd gotten word that Avery suffered a fatal accident while on the road. It had been a closed casket service. Shortly after, Nora's doctors found another growth, "inoperable" the doctors had said. Thomas retired a year early to make his beloved wife as comfortable as possible while in hospice. He cared for her, five months of waiting on her hand and foot while he watched Nora deteriorate, withering away to nothing.

After her death Thomas became a shut-in, kept the blinds closed to keep sunlight out of their home. He occasionally spoke to some of the other retired folks in the neighborhood when they tried to drop by, but only with the door cracked slightly open, never letting anyone in.

Every now and then he would call Mary. She used to love when her dad called. Ever since her brother and mother died though, the only times he would call was to tell her something was coming for him. He didn't know what it was or what it looked like, but all the same he knew it was coming and he would lose everyone he held dear. Mary believed the grief had triggered some kind of senility, told him isolation was making him paranoid.

Six months after burying Nora, and after much persuasion, his daughter finally got Thomas to agree to move in with her family. Mary hoped he would get better being around other people. He didn't. Thomas still spent most of his days holed up in their guest room. There was a big argument one day when he broke apart the coffee table to board up his windows. This was the last straw; Francis had demanded Thomas be examined. Begrudgingly, he agreed to see a physician. It wasn't dementia.

Only a few days after that doctor visit, Thomas had stood at his daughter's back door, frozen, finally seeing this figure that had filled him with dread for months. He could do nothing; icy fear froze his limbs in place. He watched the bloodbath unfold before him and wished he hadn't been right.

Now here he was, alone, crying for the loved ones he lost. Crying at feeling so helpless. His crying was cut off, however, by the sound of a loud crash. Whatever this thing was, IT was breaking down the door.

Thomas hugged his knees and watched as splinters exploded from the door. The featureless silhouette of a face peered in from the hole IT had created. On seeing Thomas (*could* IT even see without eyes?) IT began to tear at the boards barring the door.

"What are you!?" Thomas shouted as a fresh spike of terror lurched in his chest and straightened his spine. The thing didn't respond. In fact, IT didn't make a sound at all. Only the crunching of wood could be heard.

"You took them all!" Thomas began to weep again, "Now you're here for me."

Thomas stood and stared at the gaping hole where the door once was. Now in its place stood the silhouette, just the hastily hammered wood scraps barring the way. IT did not pant, IT did not breathe, IT did not move.

Thomas moved. He went through the kitchen and picked up the oil lamp he'd left there on the floor. The thing was still ripping at the boards when he returned. IT was nearly through. Thomas backed himself to the fireplace.

"Nothing can be done," he murmured, a calmness stealing over him. Thomas dropped to his knees.

The figure tossed the heavy couch to the side like it was nothing. IT slowly approached. Thomas took a deep breath before his final attempt to fight IT. He smashed the oil lamp between them, hard, instantly setting the cabin ablaze as the piles of wood scrap ignited.

The roaring fire illuminated the dark snowy night as the flames reflected off pristine blankets of white. A single scream could be heard from the cabin. Just one.

The wood crumbled as the place collapsed on itself, but nothing left the rubble. The snow continued to fall ever so elegantly as the fire, in time, slowly burned out.

The Well

Nathaniel Pizzulo wasn't very happy his mother had moved them from the fun city life to a little nowhere town outside of Roanoke, Virginia. He was just about to start middle school and had been looking forward to hanging out in the city with his friends soon. If he made friends.

Well, not gonna happen. Instead, Nate would have to start fresh. A new state, a new town, and a new home. A home surrounded by trees, dirt, and nothing.

Nate wasn't happy about his mother in general. Don't get me wrong, he cared for his mom, just not once she got to her bottle. It was funny, Nate vaguely recalled how his mother would give him a bottle to soothe him. Quiet him down. He'd outgrown that bottle for several years now. That was something for babies. But here was his mom, middle-aged and all, but still threw tantrums and needed the support of her bottle.

Although hers was different. It seemed to soothe her at first. She certainly was snappy, even cranky, until the moment she got to recline back on her couch with a bottle in hand. However, the more she drank from it, the more her temper would get out of hand. And Nate seemed to always be on the receiving end of her scorn.

He did not want to be subjected to that. Trapped in this house with her, miles from the next home, when she got like that. So Nate spent his summer in the backyard, which was mostly just yellowing grass enclosed by a brown fence. He would run around playing with sticks, pretending they were swords, or sit out there and read his old comics. Sometimes he would just lay in the dry grass and look up at the clouds and the trees that surrounded the property. The droning of cicadas carried him away in daydreams of being anywhere but home.

Finally, on one especially hot day when he was desperate for the shade of the trees, he decided to explore the woods behind their property. After stepping past the fence, he saw a path that led away from the house. Nate stood, head cocked to one side, and chewed at his bottom lip, considering. He hadn't noticed this path until now, which he guessed shouldn't have been strange. After all, this place was still new to him. After some internal struggle, the promise of an escape from the sun won out. He started down the path.

Nate heard the cheerful bird calls in the trees. That was one perk of this new home; he had never known so many birds, at least not in real life. Nate had certainly learned of different types of birds in school, and sometimes he would see them on the animal shows on TV, but the only birds he ever saw with his own eyes were pigeons. "Rats with wings," his mother called them.

Here in the country, there were red birds, blue birds, and brown ones. They were small and chirping or big with resonating caws. They watched from the trees. Some flew away as the young boy came walking by. Nate even saw a squirrel run up a nearby tree. He laughed at the funny noises it made as it flicked its fluffy tail from side to side. Cute, it was! It was nothing like the fat creepy rats with their naked wormlike tails he was used to seeing running down alleyways.

The canopy was so thick overhead a darkness seemed to seep into the wood as he walked further down the path. Nate was reminded of the skyscrapers downtown that seemed to block out the sun. It was midsummer, but the air out here felt cool and refreshing. Twigs snapped and dry leaves crunched under his step, but there weren't many of those in his way. He sought out the fallen leaves on the path to crunch them purposefully, giggling each time he did. The firm dirt path he followed was mostly clear. Inviting.

The further Nate followed the path, the more the air chilled, raising the hairs on his neck and pimpling his flesh. He was surprised to find he needed to rub his hands over his arms, gaining warmth through the friction. Nate would never have dreamed he might need to grab his little red sweater; it was such a scorchingly hot day out in the backyard. He had no idea the trees could create their own climate.

The path led out of the wood up ahead. Nate could see the light of day in a clearing just beyond and something that was centered in it. It was too far away to tell from where he stood. He walked towards it, eager to get out of the canopy and into the sunshine again. But as he stepped out from the shade of the trees, he noticed he still felt rather cold. Nate told himself he'd just been in the chill of the forest for too long. He'd warm up soon enough, surely.

Once he was out in the open, he saw it was an old well in the center of the clearing. It looked derelict, made of gray crumbling stone. A wooden roof hung over the well and this too betrayed its age. The wooden shingles were covered in moss and rot, and some of them were missing altogether.

There was something about this old well though. Nate had never seen one before and his curiosity drew him in. He hardly noticed his feet bringing him towards it, nor did he register that the nearer he approached the colder the air became.

The edge of the well met Nate's chest. He pulled himself up to look inside, feet dangling just above the dead grass encircling the well. Peeking over, he saw it was black as pitch, betraying the depth of the well. It must have been a long descent to the underground spring where people once collected water from a bucket on a pulley. A bucket that no longer seemed to exist, for the rope on the pulley was cut, idly dangling just above the maw of the well.

Nate paid no mind to the missing bucket. He wasn't there to retrieve any water. Instead, he did as any child would.

"Hellooooo" he shouted, but to his disappointment his voice was lost within the abyss and there was no echo to greet him in return.

Nate did not give up. "Hellooooo!" he shouted again, but again, nothing. He started to get upset.

"Please work!" he shouted, tears welling up in his eyes.

"Please!" he shouted once more. Nate began to cry and said softly to himself, "I just wanted someone to talk to me." Tears fell from his eyes, dripping into the depths below. He made one final attempt.

"I need you!"

"Hello," a voice said back to him. Nate gave a skeptical glare down the chute. That was not what he had said, that was not his echo returning his call. It didn't even sound like his own voice. It was soft, sweet.

"Hello," the voice said again, "isn't someone there?" It sounded innocent, like that of a child. Perhaps a little girl?

"Who's down there?" Nate asked.

"Didn't you say you needed me? Can you tell me again?" the little girl's voice said.

"I don't know who you are."

"I am here for people who need me. Don't you need me?"

"Why would I need you?"

"I can help those with a need."

"Like a genie?" Nate asked.

"Something like that, but I need to be sure... I need to hear you say it," the voice became rasped.

"Ok, yes, I need you!"

"Thank you." The voice changed, its tone became fuller, as if the girl had aged. "Who has hurt you?"

"What?! H-how do you know that?"

"Your tears. A young boy, all alone. These are tears of pain." There was something off about the voice, it fluctuated with every word. Was it a lady speaking or was it a man? Nate couldn't tell.

"It's my mom..."

"She hurts you?"

"Yes. She hurts herself too."

"Do you want her to stop hurting?"

"Yeah..."

"Would you like to stop hurting? Discover secret pleasures?"

"Of course!" His eyes were eager and his grip on the stone edge tightened, palms becoming clammy.

"Say it, please, say I want my mother to stop hurting *forever.* Say I want to experience the greatest pleasures of the Universe." The voice grew soft again, trusting.

"I want my mom to stop hurting, forever. I want to experience the greatest pleasures of the Universe!"

"Yes, oh yes!" The voice fluctuated again. Air began whispering past Nate as it was pulled down into the well.

"That's it?" Nate asked. He didn't feel cold anymore, in fact he felt a little feverish. "I don't need to say I wish?"

"No, but I have just one more favor to ask. Can you do me one more favor?"

"Yes, anything! Anything you want!"

"Give me a name… I need a name." The voice grew old and harsh, "Without a name I will die and then I cannot help you."

"Um, I don't even know if you're a boy or a girl. You're a girl, right?"

"Sure– yes! Anything. Any name will do… but hurry… I must have a name." The voice grew weaker and weaker still.

The air pulled harder into the well, tussling his hair as he leaned in.

Nate racked his brain, trying to think of names. *What's a good name? A name that would fit?*

"I know! Angel! Angel can be for a girl or a boy!"

"Oh, how fitting... Say it again..."

"I choose Angel! You will be my Angel, make mom stop hurting, make *me* stop hurting."

"Once more... just the name, quick!"

"Angel!"

With that, all the wind pulling into the well stopped and a gust of air exploded out, knocking Nate off the well and onto the ground. The only thing that followed was blackness.

Nate woke up sometime later. Hours later. The sun was no longer overhead. He looked around. He was alone. Nate pulled himself up to look inside the well again and called out.

"Hello? Angel?"

Angel did not respond, instead it was his echo. Finally, Nate got the echo he had been so pressed to hear, but that was no longer what he was hoping for. He'd hoped his new friend would speak to him once more. Nate's heart sank, realizing the whole thing must have all been in his mind. A desperate delusion of loneliness.

He realized the sky was starting to show a little purple, and lightning bugs were beginning to twinkle at the edge of the clearing. It would be dark soon and even more so within the thick canopy. He would have to hurry if he wanted to keep from getting stuck out here in the dark. Besides, if he wasn't home before dark, his mom would be upset. Well, more upset than usual.

Nate ran out of the clearing towards the path. A path that had previously been well-kept and clear earlier that day. Now it was different. The grass and undergrowth were tall, overgrown, and leaves and twigs littered the ground. If Nate didn't know any better, he would say this was no path at all. Luckily, he could still make out the impression of footsteps in the direction of the clearing by the flattened grass and snapped twigs he'd left in his wake.

Now Nate moved with purpose. He *had* to make it home before dark! Many more twigs snapped, and leaves crunched beneath his steps through the wood, but this time Nate was not laughing. It was dusk now, but under the trees it was nearly dark as night. Thankfully it wasn't chilly like it'd been before. Somehow on this return trip the warm summer air had reached below the canopy, despite the late hour.

He made it to the little fence surrounding his yard. Nate flipped the latch and quickly closed the gate behind him, letting out a sigh of relief. He darted across the yard and up the steps to his house. Nate stopped dead in his tracks once he reached the door, however. It was ajar.

Nate knew he couldn't have left the door open. His mother definitely didn't do it. Even in her most drunken state she always closed the doors. His mom despised having any doors left open, which was exactly why he was so sure he'd closed it behind him.

"Hello?" Nate slowly pushed the door wider. His mom did not respond. *Good*, he thought, *maybe she fell asleep early*. The booze did that sometimes and maybe, just maybe, he was being paranoid about the door. Maybe she checked if he was out back and didn't close the door all the way by mistake as she went back to her drink.

Nate crept in; he didn't want to wake her. Waking up his mother from a drunken nap was just as bad as getting caught out after dark. He passed through the kitchen, tile flooring so there was no worry of creaky floorboards here. When Nate reached the threshold into the dining room, he paused. He could see the blue glow of the TV from the living room gently illuminating their dining table. He hoped his mom was asleep, there was no sound for him to hear.

He stepped into the dining room. Here it was hardwood and Nate stepped ever so lightly in case there were any loose boards, not knowing this new house well enough yet. He moved around the table and stood by the wide arching threshold to the living room. The couch was in front of the TV. Something about the soft indistinct murmur he could hear from his mother's program set his nerves on edge. He could see his mother's legs dangling off the armrest.

Something was caught in his throat, a dry hard lump of panic. He tried to swallow against it as he walked up slowly and peeked over the couch. Nate screamed and fell backwards, hitting the hardwood floor with a thud.

His mother did not stir at this outburst. She lay there just as Nate had seen her, with her chest torn open, ribcage splayed out like an opened clamshell. There was a hole where her heart should be. Her eyes were missing too, with blood running down the sides of her face.

"No! No!" Nate screamed. His mom may have been very abusive to him and maybe he didn't exactly "love" his mother, but this was not a sight anybody would want to see of their parent. He didn't get up from the floor, *couldn't* get up from the floor. That's when a large shadow, unnaturally cold, loomed over him.

Nate tried to scream again but found he had lost his voice. He was petrified, unable to make a sound and frozen where he lay. Gooseflesh pimpled across his arms and the hairs on his neck rose.

The thing standing before him was unlike anything he had ever seen. Nate blinked his eyes twice, hard, as if the monstrosity in his living room was just an optical illusion. He blinked twice and then did not dare blink once more; his eyes grew wider as the realization sank in that what he saw was real.

Its slimy body was covered in an assortment of eyes, each shifting and blinking independently. A thick, mucus-like coating oozed from its crimson skin, droplets spattering as they hit the ground. Nate was disgusted, almost much as he was afraid. One of its hands held onto the couch, wickedly sharp claws piercing the upholstery. Another pressed into the ceiling as several more hands reached out towards Nate. In his mind Nate was screaming, but in reality, he still remained mute with fear.

It came closer and closer still. Nate's nostrils flared from the foul stench billowing out of its mouth, if you could call that jumble of jagged teeth a mouth. Its slippery green tongue licked the sharp spikes of its teeth. Its knees bent unnaturally backward for a two-legged creature. With each step, it left a three-toe footprint of the discharge that oozed over its body.

The Well

"Leave me alone!" Nate, at long last, shouted.

"Oh, my boy," its multiple eyes blinked as it spoke. Its voice was the voice of many. A legion. "This is what you asked me for. This is what you wanted. You are free now from this woman. Free... to come with me. I will show you the greatest pleasures unimaginable, from now until the end of eternity."

With inhuman speed the creature snatched up the young boy from the floor, its many hands wrapping around him as Nate screamed with a sound his little body had never before produced. A scream so loud his voice cracked from the strain in his larynx. A scream that traveled outside of the walls of his new house and into the woods. A scream that would have been the very last sound anyone ever heard from Nathaniel Pizzulo, had his new house in the country not been miles from the nearest listening ear.

Death Valley

"Days!? You're saying it's been *days!?*" Ziggy laughed right at me like I was some kind of clown at a five-year-old's birthday party.

The sound echoed all through the tunnel, which was lit only by the headlamp strapped to my best friend's bobbing forehead. The reverberation of his laugh was still echoing when he followed his mocking with, "Try *hours*, my man. *Hours.*"

"I don't know man..." I feigned a smirk to humor him, staring at him with one eye squinted and my right hand outstretched to block the light shining directly at my face. "I'm exhausted. We managed to nap or maybe it was sleep 'cause it definitely felt like a long-ass time to me. *That* felt like hours."

"I told ya not to sleep so much," Ziggy turned forward and continued further into the tunnel. "Come on, let's get outta here."

Let's get outta here. I repeated the phrase over and over in my head. It was such a strange concept, to just "get out," like it was that easy. You see, despite what my best friend may seem to believe, I was certain we'd been lost for days.

***

It all started on April 18th, my thirtieth birthday. Ziggy had planned a whole great adventure for us doing his two favorite activities: partying and exploring.

We had spent our first night out west in the cliche City of Sin, Las Vegas. That part was mainly for Ziggy. There was gambling (from Ziggy), there was losing (also Ziggy), and there was lots of alcohol and blow (for the both of us). It'd been ages since I let loose like that.

We stayed up most of that night, finishing off the overpriced baggie of blow and just goofing off while watching flicks back at the similarly overpriced hotel. Early in our night while we were in a more coherent state, Ziggy managed to score some acid from some guy at one of the casinos. This was the part we truly were waiting for.

After a measly two hours of something adjacent to sleep, it was now the 19th, Bicycle Day, and the start of our journey. With my birthday so close to Bicycle Day, it had always been a dream of ours to replicate that very first acid experience by dropping some of our own and going off on a psychedelic bicycle ride. It'd only taken over a decade from our early experimental days to finally make it happen, or close to it. You know how I said Ziggy seeks out the bigger thrills? Well, instead of our teenage dream of tripping and biking through a nice countryside, he'd planned out this exploration of the iconic Death Valley.

Apparently, Ziggy had met some hiker while out on a trail one afternoon. The guy had been hanging out at one of Ziggy's favorite spots, a scenic overlook where he usually liked to have a smoke. They got to sharing their favorite hiking experiences over a joint, and the man asked if Ziggy had ever been out west. He hadn't; neither of us had ever left the east coast. The hiker told him about Death Valley. How tourists go to conquer the mountains, but the real adventurers explore them, seeking out the labyrinth-like caves underground. There were even legends of an underground city out there, but through all the centuries no explorers had ever managed to bring back proof. He gave Ziggy coordinates to start exploring.

So, this was my birthday, early in the morning driving away from Vegas and a night of debauchery. We split a single dose of the paper so that we could enjoy ourselves but also be coherent enough in this brand new and desolate environment. We still saw the sights; it was difficult to get through the desert to the mountains without stopping by the tourist traps along the way.

I did love the Badwater Basin. It was fascinating to see this vast open desert seemingly covered in snow. Even with my shades on, the reflection of the sunlight off the crystalline minerals was blinding. Just like when you step outside in the morning after a heavy snowfall, when there is no longer any overcast to protect your corneas from the blazing ball of fire in the sky.

"I dare you to taste it," Ziggy taunted me after one too many times of me comparing the salt to snow.

Now, I definitely knew better, but sometimes you just have that one friend you can't seem to let down. I scooped up a handful of the ancient salt and reluctantly placed the tip of my tongue right into it.

YUCK!

I would've hurled, if my face hadn't puckered up so tight that I'd swear all anyone could see of me was my lips. It gave us a real good laugh, especially when a concerned mother attempted to shield her children's eyes from our antics.

Our GPS was a definite godsend because in that slight tripping state I could've been lost in the desert for hours. I could see in my almost childlike, drug-induced mindset how I would have laid right down on the ground and made salt angels, extending the illusion I was playing in the snow while in a t-shirt in one-hundred-degree weather. But the steady beeping from Ziggy's device kept us both focused on the journey ahead.

Our trajectory was towards Funeral Peak and as we approached the mountain range, we gazed up at the rock formations. Ziggy stood there while I walked ahead and started up the trail.

"Not quite!" Ziggy grabbed onto my pants leg just before I was out of reach.

"What?" I just stared down at him, "I'm trying to see the valley."

"We've seen valleys, my dude."

Ziggy gestured for me to come down and he started walking off to the left. I got off the trail and watched as he climbed over some rocks and headed south, parallel to the mountain range. I didn't think much of it. This was how we hiked. So I followed.

We climbed over these wondrous rock formations with such a variety of colors. It seemed as if we were going up for a time, then we started heading downhill. Down and down we climbed, until Ziggy found the spot.

"Here it is, here it is!" he announced and stepped to the side to reveal a hole.

The hole was small enough to make me feel uncomfortable at first glance, but as I eyed it over I saw we could easily fit in there, though we would have to crouch.

"I don't know," I said to him, not hiding my skepticism.

"This is what we're here for." He playfully shoved me.

"I mean…" I had to take a deep and slow breath before I could continue, "I'm still tripping."

"Pshh!" He waved his hand dismissively, "So am I!"

"I'm tripping and it looks dark in there."

"That's why I have these."

He unslung his backpack and rummaged through his stuff. He tossed a small handheld flashlight at me while he fixed the elastic band of a headlamp around his head. When he clicked it on the bulb glared right into my face. Thankfully with my shades plus the hours we'd spent out on this very sunny day, it didn't faze me – much.

"After you then," I encouraged him, and we entered.

That was April 19th.

I can't be sure at what point the acid wore off as we explored the cave. Seeing literally nothing but the backside of my best friend who was only in sight because of my flashlight was a pretty sobering thing. If something like that could "sober" you up from a psychedelic. Still felt its pleasantness trying to hold onto the curves in my grin, but my nerves were overshadowing anything else. Just before I could get claustrophobic though, the darkness ahead opened.

"Wow!" our voices echoed in unison. We looked all around us, shining our beams into the crevices of this cavern. It was quite the sight to behold – at least from what we *could* see – and for sure the end of our journey. At least that was my hope.

Once our "wow" finally stopped echoing I could make out a faint sound also reverberating off the cavern walls. That leaky faucet sound that keeps you up at night, but in a place like this it is music. I set my bag down and sat on a stone to rest up while Ziggy found a small puddle of water dripping off a stalactite. The leaky faucet.

I laid back as much as I could and closed my eyes for a moment. I could hear splashes of water and the pleasurable sounds Ziggy made while I could only assume he was washing his face. It was perfect. The hundred-degree temperature could not penetrate these caverns. It was safe to say it was a healthy seventy degrees down here. Just cool enough to provide some sanctuary from the desert heat.

It was so peaceful and perfectly quiet. Well, not completely quiet. There was the echoing drip, and Ziggy's splashing, and then the sound of air as if fleeing from a tire. A hiss… a *snake!*

"Oh shit!" I stood up instantly.

"You alright man?" Ziggy's light shined in my direction, in my face again, actually. This time it hurt my eyes.

"Hey, knock that off," I held my hand up. "Don't blind me, there's a snake in here!"

"A snake?" The light moved off my face and went searching around my feet, then over to the area I was sitting at before it made its way back to my face again. "Ain't no snakes in here, brother. They'd be too cold in here."

39

I guess he did have a point.

"Still tripping?" I could hear the humor in his voice even with his face obscured behind the light on his head.

"I guess so," was all I could think to say. I wasn't tripping, but why would a snake be all the way in here?

"Well let's get moving before any more snakes come get ya." Ziggy picked up his things and approached me.

"Nah I don't wanna leave yet, we just got here."

"Who said we leavin'?" Ziggy's headlight shone toward a different part of the cavern revealing another tunnel. "Let's see how far this place goes."

We kept going down winding tunnels that seemed to grow bigger, then smaller, as we went through. At times it was perfectly fine. I could walk straight up like a regular person and it was fun. At other points we were so crammed and so crouched I wasn't sure if we should even continue forward, but try telling Ziggy to stop an adventure. It wasn't so bad though. Right as the tight space would get to its worst, it opened back up again.

We trekked for what felt like hours. I knew for sure we were far from our starting point by now, my feet told me we had been walking on the hard stone floor of the caves for at least ten miles. By the time we reached another cavern, I began to worry it'd be night by the time we got out of the caves.

I was so grateful to get to a spot where I could rest again that I didn't even question the amount of time we had spent walking. Maybe it wasn't as long as it felt. We still had plenty of water and hadn't even begun to start on the snacks.

I was about to take a bite of a very soggy cashew butter and blackberry preserves sandwich (twist on a classic) when Ziggy called me over.

"Yo, you gotta check this!"

Before I got up, I looked around for his beam of light first to find his direction, then shone my flashlight along the ground to pick out a path through the rocks and made my way over there. Ziggy was staring at a wall.

"Come on man, I can't see this very well with my headlamp."

"I'm coming, I'm coming!" I shouted over to him. The last couple of syllables I uttered revealed the intensity of my annoyance.

"Now that you're close, I'll turn my light off." With a click, the dominance of light in the cavern switched to my hand and I pointed the light between us. I looked at Ziggy while he continued to stare at the wall.

"Cool!" he said and took the flashlight from me. He angled the beam of light towards the bottom of the wall to better illuminate the area. "Take a look."

I took a step forward and turned to face whatever he had been staring at. Cast into stark relief from the flashlight's beam, I could distinctly see carved into the stone was a circle with two vertical lines coming off the top of the circle.

"Cave paintings," Ziggy whispered.

"What does it mean?" I wasn't necessarily asking Ziggy, he knew as much as I, but it was still a question that needed to be said aloud.

"Yo, you have any idea what we just discovered!?" I could see a kind of craze come over Ziggy's eyes. "Nobody knows this is here, people don't just leave cave paintings behind for schmucks like us to find."

"Should we take a picture?" I fished my phone out of my pocket. The light was bright enough to hurt my eyes when I unlocked it. The top corner flashed with the bars, trying its darndest to find a signal. Then suddenly it went black.

"Shit, your phone die?" Ziggy thrust the flashlight back into my hands, was already reaching for his phone.

"Guess so." I held down the power button hoping it would turn back on. "There's obviously no service in here so my phone probs been draining itself searching for a signal."

"Womp womp," Ziggy made the classic 'misfortune' tone as he held up his phone, the screen similarly black. "Probably shoulda kept our phones off."

"Maybe we should turn back now." I began to step away, but Ziggy clasped a very firm hand onto my shoulder.

"We know how to get back, brother, we don't need phones for that, but what are we gonna do about our find?"

"We get out and find the park rangers and tell them what we found."

"That's it? Just some circle with lines? That ain't much for them to go on. This could just be coincidence."

"It is a clearly man-made circle. That's not natural."

"That's what they're gonna say to us though. We don't have proof. We gotta find something more, man, there's s'posed to be all kinds of wild shit down here, like mummies and treasure and shit. Let's find something that would get them to come down here and pay us!"

Ziggy faced alongside the wall towards yet another tunnel. He turned his light back on and continued down the abyss. He did not say a word to me. His action was commanding enough. I shone my light back to where we came from, in the process revealing various other tunnels. I had no choice but to grab my things, sandwich in hand, and follow.

***

Over time the twists and turns had disoriented me. It got so tight we were crawling on our hands and knees. It was not pleasant. The way the tunnel curved was so bizarre, I had no idea which way was up or whether we were even moving in the right direction. We'd been walking for dozens of miles, I thought. I just kept following the light ahead of me.

I couldn't speak for Ziggy; he was way too determined. He did not complain how hard the stone was on his knees like I had, he did not mention any sense of vertigo setting in. In fact, he did not make a single sound. I almost thought this all might have been a dream, feeling a sense of delirium. Maybe it was the acid? No, couldn't be. I had even slept in one of the small caverns we passed through. That was hours ago (or *days!?*) I couldn't fathom the amount of time we had spent here anymore, but I certainly didn't think it could still be the 19th. We had no cellphones and my watch had stopped moving at 6 o'clock on the dot.

"Need... to stop." I said at one point. My head throbbed with a rhythmic pounding like a tribal drum. I almost thought the sound was coming from further down the tunnel, but it had to be from my own exhaustion. I wasn't much for words anymore, I did my best between the wheezing and huffing from my exhaustion. It was a failed attempt.

Ziggy continued crawling forward and I continued to follow. I could feel the stone beneath me become wet. There was a trail of something ahead that we were following and crawling over. I could feel its slight stickiness between my fingers. I wiped the moisture onto my shirt and aimed my light at it. Streaks of crimson. Looking down for the source of the wetness I saw a trail of red splotches, some in the shapes of hands. It was Ziggy's blood. His skin was getting worn down from the crawl.

I screamed at the sight. There was no way he could have been wearing himself down that much. I stopped moving and began to freak out, swearing up a storm. What knocked me back to my senses was Ziggy shaking me. Shaking the sense back into me, although he was hardly the person for such a job.

"Dude, it's alright," he reassured me. "It's alright! We're here."

"Here?"

I felt sick. Where was "here"? There hadn't been a destination we sought. Only the prospect of something valuable. I opened my eyes and at first, I wasn't comforted at all. The sight that greeted me was the crazed eyes of the man who was once my best friend. I say that because the look within his eyes was one I had never seen. They say the eyes are the windows into a person's soul. His windows opened into a black empty room.

Beyond Ziggy, though, was a different kind of sight. Light. We had reached an end to this bizarre journey and made our way out of the cavern. Thank goodness!

"Come on," Ziggy said before he jogged away towards the light.

I followed. I could feel air coming in through the opening. It was such a relief, but only for a moment. The air was stale and foul. It smelled of sulfur and was definitely not what I wanted for my first breaths outside of this cave.

The light outside was odd, unnerving. The sky was a rusted orange color, and not a single speck of blue anywhere. Possibly it was approaching dusk? I didn't have much time to focus on that though. The sight before me was some kind of undocumented wonder.

"Whoa!" We were both in awe as we reached the edge of a cliff and stared at the deep canyon before us.

"That drop is almost endless!" I shouted down into the vast space between where we stood and the other side of the canyon. My words echoed before they were lost in the immense depths that were faintly illuminated with an orange glow.

"What do you think is down there? Lava?" I asked Ziggy but he did not look down. He just stared out at the canyon wall across the chasm.

"That's a very strange marking," I said to him. Still no response. "It's almost perfect. Like the letter V. Two of them." I held out my right hand with my fingers like a peace sign, forming a V, then I placed two fingers from my other hand sideways over them to replicate the marking before us.

"We're here," Ziggy said once again, and I followed his stare.

His eyes were fixed, not on the canyon wall nor the large perfectly straight angles of the marking, but focused directly at the center of the strange lines. In its center was a hole. It was unlike any natural hole one might find in a wall. This was a void.

I could feel the void like a knot burrowing deep within my chest. It was consuming me. Consuming my soul. I wanted nothing more than to turn back, get away from this place. I would take my chances back within the caverns, anything. I couldn't. Something tugged at me as the sensation grew from my chest and spread throughout my body.

I looked over to Ziggy, but he was no longer there. I saw him further off to the right where the land we stood on seemed to curve like a large basin, connecting to the opposite side of the canyon. It would make for easy travel to the cliff's edge above the symbol, and that terrifying hole.

Once again, I followed after Ziggy. My pace had no urgency, I walked in a trance. The path towards the other side crossed over what seemed like a dried-out stream that had perhaps flowed into the depths of the canyon many eons ago. After a bit of a scramble, I climbed back up and was on the flat surface once again.

Ziggy had already made it to the precipice above the strange markings. I wasn't far behind. He stood there, frozen, and glanced over at me. His eyes were hollow, soulless. A man I had known for the majority of my life looked right past me, as if I weren't even there. I couldn't blame him. I felt as if I wasn't there at all. This couldn't have been real.

Ziggy began to climb down as I neared the cliff's edge. I gazed out across the canyon to the cavern we had crawled out of. Its darkness was not of the same intensity as the hole below. I again looked down to the depths of the chasm below and felt mesmerized by the faint glow at the very bottom. Finally, I looked at the cliffside below us and watched as Ziggy made his way down, following the unnaturally precise grooves in the rock that formed this strange marking. He stopped at the hole.

Ziggy looked up at me one last time. His skin was ashen and his lips were pale gray. This adventure had taken the life out of someone I had always known to be larger than life. That final look he gave me, at first glance I thought it was the same emotionless one, but just maybe there was a hint of sorrow there. He crawled into the dark hole.

Now it had become my turn to approach. No, this was not what I wanted. I thought about turning back around. I even believed for a moment I was doing exactly that, but the next thing I knew I was staring into the black abyss myself. There was something about this place. Something about this hole had completely taken over me. All free will was lost.

I stared into the abyss for an unfathomable amount of time. My eyes watered from the strain. The longer I stared the more I could see this was no hole at all. There was no depth to look into, it was just solid black, empty. I heard sounds coming from this void. The vicious hissing of ferocious serpents, the clanging of metal upon metal, and the pained wailing of poor tortured souls.

As I continued staring into the void, I became aware in a detached sort of way that something wet was trickling from my eyes, running down my face. A faint greenish-yellow light appeared. It was inviting. All thoughts of resistance faded away. All thoughts of my brother, Ziggy, disappeared. All yearning to go back to my home vanished. There was just me and the light.

I reached inside.

A Hard Night's Work

It had been a long day at work, a long day of work. Andres lived alone and had two jobs just to barely make ends meet. His car payment badgered him every single month, plus there was the insurance, his phone bill, and of course rent plus utilities. There were some days between paychecks he would barely have enough money for food.

Why not get a roommate? Well, he had to leave his last place in an emergency when sharing a single bedroom with his ex didn't pan out. Andres' landlord hooked him up with another single bedroom apartment. He supposed if he were to get a roomie they could maybe use the living room as a bedroom, but for now he had the place to himself and he did his very best to keep it.

During the week it wasn't so bad, working alternating days between running the convenience store and cooking at what was once his favorite bar. However, he dreaded the weekends when both shifts aligned. His first shift started at six in the morning, selling cigarettes and junk food to the many passers-by up until four o'clock.

Andres had to scramble to clock out and rush out the door, down the boulevard, over one street and across the square, all the while changing shirts on the run, just so he could make it to his evening shift in the kitchen. He was there till two in the morning, only to collapse at home for a couple hours then get up and do it again the next day.

There was one silver lining. The parking garage just one block over from the bar was $5 all day, weekends only. This meant he could afford to drive to work and not spend an extra hour on the bus, then figure out a ride to get back to his part of town at a time of night when no public transportation was running. Besides, he liked this garage, there were no cameras or personnel to monitor which made it easier for him to smoke his morning joint before his first shift.

This happened to be a Saturday, so Andres had the luxury of parking in the garage. At the end of this long day, he was walking down the street to the garage; he'd gotten a couple drinks in him after his shift, so he was feeling mighty relieved.

He had started his day at the store doing his usual routine, trying to get through that first hour of denying the vagrants the purchase of beer before the clock hit seven. The rest of the day was rather mundane, right up until some kid puked in the candy aisle. Of course, that happened at the very end of his shift. He had to mop it up before he could leave, making him just a little late for the shift change. His kitchen manager at the bar scolded him about the importance of showing up on time, right before he jumped on the line for the dinner rush and started slinging those burgers into the late hours.

As soon as Andres was done closing the kitchen he immediately went to the upstairs bar and asked for his unusual end-of-day drink. A shot of whiskey and a beer – what a relief. Once the upstairs bar closed, Andres and the bartender went over to the bar next door that stayed open later and threw back a few more beers. They shared anecdotes of different customer interactions throughout the day.

Their duo grew as time went by and other service workers came in after their bars closed as well. Andres always loved these moments. It was a small break from the hustle of the day, giving him some sense of a personal life – even if everyone was just trying to have a drink to end their workday and there was nothing truly personal about it.

Once in the garage, Andres stumbled on his way to the little kiosk by the stairs and elevator to pay for his ticket. With the $5 flat rate he could've simply paid on his way out of the garage in the morning, but he liked the routine of paying before leaving at night. He felt like he was less likely to lose his stub during the day if he knew he still needed to pay for it.

The machine always took its sweet time turning gears to count the single five-dollar bill he inserted, and perhaps even longer to cough up the ticket. Now with that in hand Andres turned around. He faced the door to the stairwell, right next to the elevator. His car was parked only up two levels and he always preferred the stairs since the elevator was even slower than the ticket machine.

Andres pushed through the door. The moment he stepped over the threshold he jumped with a start. There was a man only a couple feet away, just standing there on the second step, facing directly towards him.

"Oh! My bad, man…" Andres apologized for his startled reaction.

Andres looked up at the man; he wasn't any less startling on second glance. The man stood rigidly, uncannily silent and still. He wore black boots, black jeans, black leather gloves, and a black hoodie. Andres had spoken to the man before getting a good look at his face, or what little of it was visible. Though it was past two in the morning by now, this guy wore dark sunglasses and a black baseball cap with the hood up over it.

The man still hadn't moved, nor acknowledged Andres in any way. This was unsettling enough, but there was something more. Although most of this man's appearance was covered, it was what Andres could see of his face that sent a chill through him like an icy hand gripping his spine.

The man's face wasn't just clean-shaven, it had not a speck of stubble, seemingly pore-less. His nose was unnaturally triangular and smooth as well. Andres looked at the brow just above the man's black shades. No eyebrows. The only part exposed from his hat and hood setup was his temples, which suggested he was completely hairless underneath the disguise. The lack of hair wasn't the only thing that made Andres shift on his feet. There was something about his skin. It seemed smooth, too smooth, almost like latex, and the wrinkles in his neck and across his chin sat unnaturally.

Finally, the man stepped forward, taking the last two steps, and passing by Andres out the door. The instant the door shut Andres bolted up those steps, taking them two at a time. He made it to the third floor, empty save for two vehicles, a black van parked close by and his silver sedan at the far end. Andres rushed over to his car and sat for a few moments, trying to process what he had seen. He was just about to text his best friend about this strange encounter when he heard the shrill squeak of the door to the stairs opening.

A Hard Night's Work

It was the man in black, stepping through the doorway. Andres sank down in his seat, watching the man. He stood there for a moment then turned, looking at Andres' car. He lingered in that direction for a moment before turning his stare to the black van and slowly stepped to it. Even his movement was unnatural. Stiff.

Andres watched from inside his car and what he'd at first disregarded as just a van in the shared space now added to his unease. It was matte black, not the trendy matte finish some cars seem to have these days; this seemed old, run-down. The windows were heavily tinted, and no license plate was visible from the back.

Andres started up his engine. It was time to get the hell out of here. As Andres picked up speed towards the ramp down to the street he glanced in the rear-view mirror. He saw the man stretch out his right hand, holding something in his grasp, but he was too panicked to get a good look at it. His ears registered a suppressed bang that told him what the object was. Still some distance from the ramp, *POP!* A back tire exploded, spinning Andres out. He kept pushing his car.

The shrill sound of metal scraping across the concrete floor pierced the night as Andres fishtailed this way and that, attempting his escape. He looked up to the mirror again and saw the man advancing on him. Now he could see the gun clearly in his hand. This time he saw the flash that accompanied the silenced shot before another tire popped.

Andres snatched up his phone from the passenger seat and bolted out the door. He aimed for the stairwell but did not get far before he heard the gun's suppressed fire again. A searing pain exploded in his right knee, sending him tumbling to the floor and his phone skidding across it. The impact left skin from his elbows shredded on the concrete. He turned over and screamed as he saw the streak of blood coming from his knee, already seeping through his jeans.

Swiftly approaching was the man, the faceless man. Andres crawled on the ground to his phone. The man in black shot again. The phone exploded before Andres' tear-soaked eyes, inches from his outstretched fingers. Even though he had nowhere to go, the man placed a heavy steel-toed boot onto Andres' back, keeping him in place.

"P-please!" Andres screamed, "please don–" A final shot went off.

If you thought this was a story about how Andres needed to make ends meet, then you were mistaken. This is a story about number 132, of the Faceless, getting spotted while on assignment and how they helped Andres meet his end.

This "man in black," 132, hoisted the lifeless body up onto their shoulder and took it to the van, tossing it in the back. 132 rifled through a few items and pulled out a white gallon bottle with one hand and a red rag in the other. They splashed the contents of the bottle onto the pool of blood where the body had been. Methodically and silently, they wiped up every trace of bodily fluids, then returned these things to the van.

132 shifted the body to the side and pulled out a long sleek case. Almost like the case of an instrument, like a trombone. Almost. The Faceless were a different type of artist.

They looked at the car with the two flattened back tires, engine still running. Not a single muscle stirred in their face as they stared lifelessly through the shades. They wouldn't be able to move it, not with the two flats, but this was fine. The Port Authority would tow it later in the morning. 132 already had one inconvenience and there was still a job to do. Port Authority might find the car and deal with it, but they would never find the body.

No matter to 132, that was why they liked this garage. There were no cameras or personnel to monitor, which made it easier for 132 to get in and out.

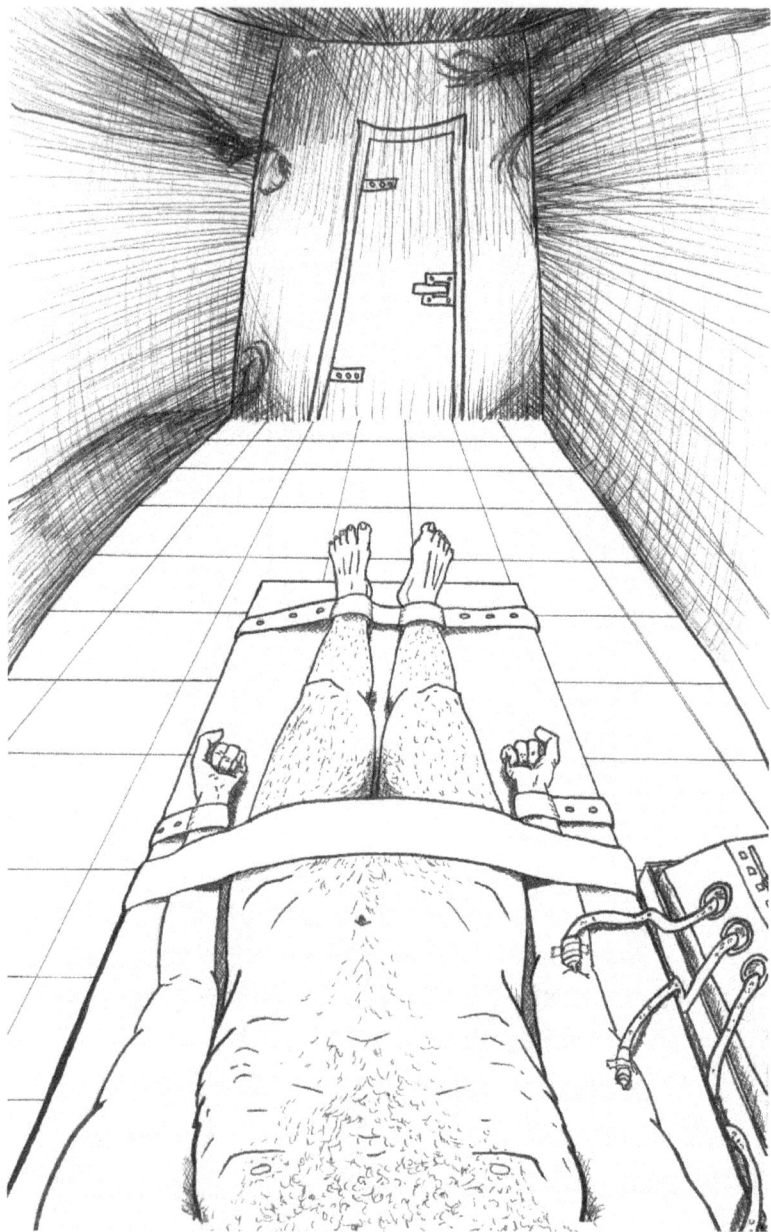

The Making of a Hero

The moment I walked through the doors into the waiting room, the smell of cleaning chemicals hit my nose. The room felt something like a doctor's office, sterile white walls, a matching polished floor. Uncomfortable metal chairs lined the perimeter of the room. Five others were already seated when I entered, scribbling down on some forms attached to a clipboard. The soldier who'd guided me to the room turned and held out a large resealable plastic bag. My name, date of birth, and the current date were already printed on it.

"Put your wallet, keys, cellphone, and any jewelry you may have into this bag," the soldier demanded, and I quickly did so.

Wallet, cellphone – double-checked to make sure it was off, though turning off all civilian communication devices had been a requirement just to enter the building – then placed that in there. No keys, since Leora took the car back, and a buckeye seed that I kept in my pocket for luck.

The man in the camo kept a stern face as he eyed my wedding ring, "Place any and *all* jewelry into the bag."

I gave a mournful sigh and reluctantly pulled off the wedding band from my ring finger. I hadn't even gotten to wear it for a full year. I noted with a pang of regret that there wasn't even a tan line on my finger yet. I held the ring up and quickly glanced at the inscription, *Forever & Always*, then gave it a little kiss before dropping it into the bag.

In one swift motion the soldier zipped the bag and handed me a clipboard with a pen and a thick stack of papers clipped to it. The door shut in my face as he departed without another word.

I chose the seat closest to me. A red-headed lady sat about three chairs to my right and a tan fellow with indigenous looking facial features was across from me. They both glanced at me as I sat and I gave them the respectful head nod of acknowledgement. The man across from me returned his eyes to his clipboard, but the lady gave a small smile. I leaned forward to look at the three other guys scattered towards the other side of the room, but none looked away from their forms.

Settling in, I got to work filling out the forms. I filled in the day's date on the top of the first sheet. The very first question, PLEASE PRINT FULL NAME:

I looked up from my paper and saw the guy sitting in the back right corner looking at me. He was a scrawny White kid, couldn't have been much older than eighteen. So, I answered my first question out loud to him, "I'm Reivaj Castillo," and flashed a friendly smile. That was me, always a friendly human.

"Uh, hey," he said, "I'm Austin."

"Texas! Great city," I joked.

"What? No, I'm not from Tex-ass." He seemed annoyed. He clearly didn't get my joke.

"No, was just thinking like Austin, Texas and we're here in Arlington and there's like, an Arlington, Texas as well."

"...Right." He still seemed very put off by it.

"Sorry, it was a joke." Probably not a good one. My jokes usually seemed to require a little too much explaining and a little too much thinking for most anyone I was telling them to.

"Yeah, whatever weirdo," Austin said underneath his breath.

"Don't be a dick, dude," an Asian man who was sitting against the back wall nearest the scrawny kid said. "He's just trying to be friendly and probs nervous. Shit, man, we all are."

"I'm not nervous. Why would I be nervous?" Austin snapped.

"Maybe because we all signed up for some super high-up confidential military science experiment and have no idea what kind of shit is in store for us," said a bearded Black man who sat on the same side of the wall as the native. "We in this together. You don't have anything to prove to any of us." Then he looked over at me. "I'm Derrick."

"Nice to meet you."

"Hey what's up, I'm Luke." The Asian man, who might have been Vietnamese, shone a great big smile my way. "I'm from here in Arlington, where you from, man?"

"Well, I'm from Greensburg, PA, but I came from Pittsburgh. That's where my wife and I live."

"Oh shit, Steeler city," said Derrick. "Just don't go into Maryland and tell them that you're a Steeler boy."

"Yeah, no I don't-"

"Hey guys, there's a lot of stuff to fill out in these forms." The redhead spoke over me, and our short-lived conversation died.

60

It was silent except for the scribbling of pen on paper, and the annoyingly loud tick-tocking from a clock that hung on the back wall. It was the one and only feature on any of the walls in the whole room.

I glanced over at the clock. It had been twenty minutes since our conversation ended and I was just starting the third page. The first two were basic. Name, date of birth, address, marital status, spouse's name. I lingered on that last part as I thought about my Leora. How she must have been crying in the car after dropping me off. Whether she went home and plopped in front of the TV to distract herself, or simply curled up in our bed to sleep off what I'm sure she hoped was a nightmare.

I went back to the forms: nationality, ethnicity, education, pretty much anything you would find on a W2. The more I filled out the more in-depth it became. Parent names, their place of birth, citizenship, family history of diseases. The next few parts were more of a personality test. Then a morality test. Being a military program, I reasoned, they must get all kinds of strange folks with questionable motives for volunteering.

An hour had passed by and most of the others seemed to have finished up their documents. I still had several more pages to go. I did arrive after everyone else, but I was always slower at official forms anyway. From taking the standardized tests in school to filling out doctor's office forms, it always seemed to take me longer than my peers.

Another 20 minutes and I was nearly finished with my packet. Just one more section, the waivers and consent. Several pages, each with more words squeezed onto them than any of the other sections. I skimmed through the tiny print, something about not liable for this or that and health conditions, next of kin – these forms are all the same. Glancing around the room, I couldn't imagine anybody reading this entire thing to the letter. I mean, we get so many "read the terms" from everything these days and it's all basically the same stuff. I scribbled my final signature at the bottom and set the clipboard down.

I looked up and noticed Luke and Derrick were quietly talking. The red-headed woman had moved down closer to them. Austin lounged back with his eyes closed, probably asleep. The native remained across from me. His arms were folded and he seemed to be resting as well until he opened his eyes, looking at me.

"Finally done?" he asked, no condescension in his tone.

"Yeah, *finally!*" I looked over at the clock, "Wow, that time just melted away."

"Sure did." He glanced over at the clock himself.

"Hey, Reivaj!" Luke waved over to me. "Now we're all done. So… when do you think they will come and get us outta here?"

"Shit if I know," Derrick snorted.

"Well, whatever," Luke shrugged, then his smile returned, "How much you wanna bet they forgot about us?"

"We don't have our wallets, moron," that brat Austin grumbled without opening his eyes.

"Haha, whatever! Hey, this is Simone," Luke gestured to the redhead.

"Hey," She waved awkwardly.

"Hello." I looked across to the man ahead of me, "So that leaves you."

"Joe." Joe extended his right hand, "You can call me Joe."

I shook his hand, "Nice to meet you. Nice to meet all of you. To be honest I was very nervous about this whole ordeal."

"I still *am*," said Simone. "We still have no clue what we are getting into."

"True, but I didn't think I'd make any friends," Luke said.

"Yeah, exactly," I agreed. "I was half afraid we were going to get sent to a bootcamp, even though we didn't exactly sign up for the Marines. Coming out here to the Pentagon, though? What a trip! Never did I imagine I would ever set foot inside of the notorious Pentagon."

"Experimental volunteers, though? I know I'm already sitting here, but at least enlisting to the Marines is kind of straightforward," Luke replied. "It makes sense they would host us at the Pentagon."

The rapport flowed naturally as we each chimed into the conversation, slowly getting to know one another. The time ticked by and still no one from the experiment had come to check on us. We shared some laughs and I almost shed some tears talking about leaving my new wife alone back home. Joe gave me some good insight though. He told me how we all must make some sacrifices for our loved ones and sometimes they may seem especially challenging, but when done for the right reasons it'll help you through.

Just as a natural lull fell in the conversation, I could hear the *clack-clack* of footsteps approaching the door. The click of the door unlocking caused us all to look up expectantly. I hadn't realized we were locked in.

The handle turned and the door pushed open. A man in green camo held open the door while a much older fellow stepped in. Clearly a high-ranking officer, he wore a neatly pressed formal military uniform. His breast was decorated with all kinds of pins, a pair of wings, and two medals. He had three stars on each shoulder, and on top of his short gray hair he wore the white Marine Corps hat.

"Alright, listen here. I am General Hawkes; you will refer to me as Sir." His voice had the tone of someone used to being listened to instantly, no matter what room he was in.

He scanned the room. All of us directed our attention to him, even Austin. "You have done well by remaining in the room, getting to know each other, and not attempting for a single moment to leave – we have a camera in the clock. You all passed the first test of patience. That is good. If you do not have patience for this program, then we do not have patience for you.

"Now, if you follow me and Private Mahoney over here, we will turn in your forms and begin debriefing you on why you are here and the nature of the war we are in. Russia is at it again, but this time they've got China with them. It's a Cold War all over again, and now we're in a race to achieve the perfect super soldiers."

***

We had each already received the standard issue military buzz down to the skull. It was sad to see Simone's gorgeous red locks piled around her sneakers. Same with Joe's silky black strands. They didn't make much of a fuss though, good champs. Well, I could see the hurt slightly water up in Simone's golden eyes. Derrick's cut had been quick since his head was practically shaven anyway. Luke just repeatedly let out a quiet string of, "Oh fuck, man," each time the sheers buzzed over his dome.

Austin, on the other hand, was the worst, to no one's surprise. He fidgeted and jumped up constantly. They had to have someone hold him down. His hair wasn't even that long! I knew then that he wouldn't make the cut. I just didn't realize that would be my final memory of poor young Austin, obnoxiously whining as a river poured from his eyes over his short blonde hair, crying for his mommy.

After we got our new hairdos, or lack thereof, we were marched down an uncomfortably bright corridor. Walls, ceiling, and floors were white just like the waiting room and the barber shop. The white corridor led to a darker one ahead. After crossing the threshold, I noted the floors were concrete. These walls were a mildewy off-white and the lights above flickered and buzzed here and there.

I had only just met these guys, but already I felt we were in this together. They were decent people and I'd really enjoyed talking with them. I could sense the collective disappointment wash over our little squad when our march down the long hall ended at a row of doors. Partly because we knew just by seeing the row of six doors that it could only mean separation. And partly because, by the looks of the doors, we could see this wasn't going to be a walk in the park. Oh, did I say disappointment? I meant to say we were *terrified*.

The Making of a Hero

The doors were metal and looked ominous in the dim lighting. They were once silver, but now orange cracks of rust covered the doors like an alien spiderweb. A group of armed soldiers stood behind us intimidatingly. I hadn't noticed them until that moment, I don't think any of us had. We had no choice but to enter our rooms.

As I stepped into the room on the far right, two soldiers holding M16s followed closely behind. They stood by the door and General Hawkes passed one of them a clear bag. I could see the bag that had my personal items inside of the larger bag. The door was shut, leaving me in the room with them.

Directly in front of me stood a tall metal table. I looked around the small space. I would come to know this room well over the next few days. The brown and beige brick walls, the dark ceiling with the single operating lamp above what I then recognized as an operating table, and the rusty-brown stains that speckled the yellowing square tiles of the floor. Later in my life I would come to recognize such stains as old, dried blood.

"Undress," one soldier said as the other opened the bag.

I didn't rebel. Not I had any choice in the matter. I removed my shirt, and the cold of the room instantly gave my skin gooseflesh, hardening my nipples. Next, I kicked off my shoes while unbuckling my belt. Dropping my shirt into the soldier's bag of my personal belongings, I again thought of Leora. She would have been pissed. She bought me that shirt. She said it made my arms sexier, which I found hard to believe because I had scrawny arms, but if it made her happy… God, did I miss her, now more than ever.

My pants were coming down past my knees before I realized it. They say in traumatic moments the victim involuntarily escapes, blocking moments like these from their mind. If it weren't for that instinctive defense mechanism, I probably would've heard the single cracking pop from one of the other rooms which caused the soldiers to trade looks. But again, involuntary escape. I suppose I was thinking about that as I stepped out of my pants. Had I pulled my pants down? I just remember standing there in my socks, my knees pressed together, and one arm clutched across my chest, covering my crotch with my other hand.

"Strip down all the way," barked the soldier holding the bag, gesturing for me to put *all* my clothes inside.

I peeled off my white ankle-length socks and placed them in the bag, another shock of cold shooting up my spine as my bare feet touched the tile floor. The two soldiers just stared at me, or more like they were staring passed me. I'm sure watching a man strip against his will was awkward for them as well. I knew what they were waiting for.

I took a deep breath of icy cold air. Had it been getting persistently colder? No, I was just naked, or at least I was about to be. I swiftly pulled down my red and black striped boxer briefs. Leora loved those. She had called them my pirate shorts. It was done. I was bare-ass naked, down to my birthday suit.

I dropped my underwear into the bag. The final piece! I watched the man seal it up. I caught a glimpse of the very minimal black sharpie on it. "042" is all that was printed. That is who I came to be. With the reluctant surrender of my wife's favorite pair of underwear, Reivaj Castillo was gone. At that same moment I was reborn as patient 042, or just number 42 at times.

I was told to sit on the table. I did so, instantly wincing, and simultaneously my butt cheeks clenched. If I thought the room was cold already, sitting on that slab of metal redefined the word. Every follicle on my body straightened out each individual hair. I crossed my ankles and tried to hold my feet with one another in a futile attempt to retain some warmth. I laid my hands over my junk. I was every bit of the word embarrassed, humiliated!

I sat, staring down at my whitening feet, rocking them back and forth. I kept silent. The two soldiers did as well. We were like that for what felt like a long time before I heard a metallic squeal approach then stop outside of the door. The door swung open with a rusted screech. General Hawkes stepped in, followed by a woman in a white lab coat wearing a blue surgeon's haircap who pulled in a squeaky cart. An older gentleman wearing the same outfit entered the room next, one hand pushing the other side of the cart and pulling along a wheeled IV stand behind him.

She swung the cart around to the right side of the table. The lady looked over to me as she began prepping the tools on the cart; her smooth dark face seemed almost kind. Almost. The cart held a strange machine, along with the usual tools you would find at the doctor's office. I began to take note of that machine with its three tubes but was quickly interrupted.

"Tell me, when was your last physical, Patient 042," said the male scientist. He had an accent, I believe it was Russian.

"Uh. I don't know." I tried to keep my eyes focused on the door straight ahead, looking just between the two soldiers. The

68

Russian scientist was already leaning in with some device to inspect the inside of my right ear.

"About three years ago I had my last skating accident. I went to the clinic then." He moved on to my left ear. "They did like a standard check, but an actual physical? I was probably eighteen. I don't have health insurance, so, y'know…" I trailed off.

"Ah, yes! Such a rich country, these Capitalistic States, and yet no health care is provided for the public."

"Can the political bullshit, Petrov," Hawkes snapped.

"Yes, yes, not the place." Dr. Petrov pulled out a wooden stick and a little flashlight, "Open up, please, and do not forget to say *ahh*!"

While he checked the inside of my throat, the female doctor prodded at the left side of my back, then scribbled something down. She seemed to be noting my scars. Next, she pulled up my left arm to observe the scars on my elbow. I had tumbled down a freshly paved hill from my skateboard years ago and traded some of my flesh with the pavement. It was a terrible trade.

"Anwara, check his reflexes," Petrov said, handing her the little reflex hammer. She tapped away at that uncomfortable soft spot in my right knee, then the left. Petrov pulled out his little light again and shined it into my left eye, then the right. They both scribbled down their notes.

"Your arm." Anwara waited for me to offer her my left arm, instead of just taking it this time. She then wrapped a blood pressure cuff around my elbow, slipped the end of her stethoscope underneath into the pit of my elbow, and popped in the earpieces. She began pumping, the cuff tightening nearly to the point of pain as I could feel the pulse of blood in my arm. Anwara listened intently.

"He has great blood pressure, Mikhail." She scribbled that down too, then undid the whole thing.

"Do you smoke?" Petrov (or Mikhail) asked as he put his own stethoscope into position.

"No. I mean, I used to. For almost ten years on and off. Was never a big smoker, though. A pack would last me weeks. It's been about three years."

"Good." He placed the end of the stethoscope to my back behind the left shoulder. If that thing was cold, I couldn't tell anymore. "Deep breath in." I inhaled. "Out." I exhaled. He slid it over to the other side, and we repeated the process.

"Very good." He listened to my lungs again from the front of my chest. "Yes, very good lungs."

"You are a great specimen, 42," Anwara complimented. At least, I think it was a compliment. "Very healthy."

"Yes, this one might be promising. Hopefully will make up for the loss of patient: 039." Petrov considered me for a moment. "We need to check for lumps. Would you prefer Dr. Begum to check you, or I?"

"Uh," My knees instinctually closed together, "I'm good, I checked not long ago."

"Haha, I am certain you check regularly. I hope so at least! But we must check every part of our assets ourselves. This is a very controlled experiment." He turned to the cart, snapping on a pair of purple latex gloves. "I suppose I will do it myself. Now, stand up."

I stood and put my hands to my sides. I wasn't a man with many insecurities, actually I only had one. I only liked the ladies I slept with to see my stuff. Not that I was embarrassed of what I had, I mean it wasn't anything special. But here I was in a creepy room with five strangers all watching me and one of them was cupping my testicles.

Now I knew what a prized pig might feel like getting rated at the county fair. The way they talked about me too, like I wasn't even there, like I wasn't even a person! "Asset!" "Specimen!" they called me. I had signed my dignity away and there was nothing I could do about it now. I felt so helpless.

"Okay, now cough." I coughed twice. "Good. Cough again." I did it twice again. "Okay, you check out!" Dr. Petrov discarded his gloves and then put on a new pair.

"Now for the unpleasant part. Turn around, hands on the table, firmly. Now, spread your legs and deep breath…" "Prostate seems just fine."

"Now, please, stand up straight." Dr. Begum asked and after I did, she measured the length of my shoulders. Then the circumference of my arms, my waist, my thighs, and my calves, recording each part as she moved down my body.

"Hop back on the table please," she instructed. Dr. Begum left the room and came back in shortly with another short cart containing dozens of sticky electrodes with wires all feeding into a box-shaped machine connected to a monitor screen.

After the doctor's extremely thorough examination, the table was now more uncomfortable than I thought it could ever be. But the examination was not over yet. After smearing a paste across my freshly shaved skull, Dr. Begum began sticking at least two dozen electrodes across my scalp.

"Now, lie down and close your eyes, and we will begin your baseline EEG scan, 42," Dr. Petrov informed me. The shock of the cold exam table on my bare back caused me to audibly gasp, sending a fresh wave of chills radiating across my body strong enough to make my teeth chatter.

"Please, try to relax. It is important you remain completely motionless for the duration of the scan so we can get an accurate reading of your brain waves," the Russian said. Like I could control my reactions in this ice box! A series of beeps told me the process had begun.

And with that, I heard the shuffle of the doctors retreating, leaving me with the sticky paste and wires attached to my head. Dr. Petrov and Dr. Begum began speaking quietly to each other, murmuring their observations as they compared notes. The minutes slowly crept by. Now that there were no further instructions, my mind began to wander, a new level of anxiety setting in as I considered the extensive examination I was being subjected to. What on earth would they need to measure my brain waves for?

At last, the machine gave a final prolonged beep, and Dr. Begum approached the table again, beginning the process of removing the electrodes.

"So, Number 42." General Hawkes stepped forward as the doctor continued cleaning my scalp. "As I informed this cohort earlier, we are in a race of science. The Confederation of Communist States is developing the greatest military innovation of this century." Hawkes hovered over me, still talking at me as the light above glared into my eyes, "Now, I do have to admit, there are some pretty knowledgeable scientists between the Chinese and Russians."

"Some of the greatest minds in the world," Petrov smiled. At least I think he smiled; the shadows cast over their three faces made it hard to tell.

"We don't need that horseshit, Petrov. Let me brief 'im!" Hawkes snapped.

I felt a cool swab over the veins on my right arm just before Anwara said, "You're going to feel a prick."

"Ouch!" I felt something, alright. More of a crunch, straight into the biggest vein on the inside of my elbow.

"The sneaky bastards got the jump on us," Hawkes continued, "Brainstorming, planning, and getting data together while we were recovering from the SK4-II virus *they* created."

"We developed no such thing," Petrov contradicted. He clicked a couple switches into place from the mysterious machine and hooked one of its cords into the IV bag. "I thought it was America that spread fear of the fictional pathogen. That was when your entire system changed, wasn't it?"

"Listen here, I am the one telling the history. Not your Russian propaganda."

"Well, then, maybe I should take over," Dr. Begum interjected, just before a tougher pinch pierced the muscle of my right bicep.

"You see, Dr. Mikhail Petrov was one of the top geneticists in the C.C.S. developing ways to enhance their soldiers," Dr.

Begum explained. "They discovered one serum to aid the development of muscle growth, one to sharpen reflexes, and a third to better access parts of the brain unused. Excuse me, you will feel a pressure behind your ear."

I felt my right ear pop with the crunching sound of cartilage as it burst into a piercing white noise, only for a second. Within that same second my vision burst into a blinding white then quickly cut to complete blackness before the room fuzzily came back into focus.

"The conditions I had to work in were horrible," Petrov picked up the story. "I felt threatened for my life and insecure that my work would go without recognition. So, I fled to America. That was when I met Anwara Begum here. She already had ties to the military and helped me bring light to the experiments we were beginning overseas. Unlike my C.C.S. comrades, I had the one up. I received American funding. That is how I built my machine."

The hum and steady beeping of the machine to my right caught my attention. I could see there were three cylinders of some sort of liquid within the glass case of the machine. The tubes rattled in place. There was a dial with numbers that went up to ten. Currently it was set at three. My eyes followed the tubes coming out of the side of the machine. One was connected to the IV pack feeding into my vein and the second tube led into the muscle of my bicep.

The third I couldn't see where it ended. I tried moving my head more to the right – OUCH! A searing pain bit back as my head bumped into something... oh god, that had to be what was behind my ear. I choked back a sob as the realization sunk in that I had a machine jacked into my head. Oh Leora, what did I get myself into!?

"In short, my machine here transfuses all three serums into a single asset." Dr. Petrov patted the machine gingerly. "My goal is to create one perfect super soldier."

I tried to ask him how many patients had shown results, but all I could manage to speak out was, "How many?"

Luckily, he seemed to know what I meant. It was probably a question asked often in this deranged state. He responded, "You are the forty-second experiment. None of the previous thirty-six have completed the clinical trials, so we still haven't made a successful transfusion."

"Ha-haaaav..." I was just trying to repeat the word 'haven't!' I couldn't even get myself to say that. My vision was so blurred. My muscles clenched tight. I could feel my jaw locking into place each time I tried to open it. What were they doing to me?

"Oh, all sorts of reasons... Anwara, bring in the oxygen." The third figure left my frame of vision, such as it was. "Muscular atrophy, cardiogenic shock–"

"They fucking die is what happened." That was General Hawkes. I could no longer distinguish their faces. I was having some trouble identifying their voices, but I was certain that was Hawkes. "Shit, one asset right here in this room freaked and tore the cords out from their arm and head. He collapsed and bled out.

"That is why we take the necessary precautions." The voice was far off and swimming. I did my best to lift my head. I couldn't. I just shot my gaze down my body and saw straps along my torso and arms. When had they strapped me in? I couldn't tell you. The room was spinning into a nauseating swirl.

I think the third shadowy figure returned to hover over me. They seemed to be one and many at the same time. I don't know what kind of chemicals they were pumping into me, but it was making me hallucinate. I was hearing imaginary screams of terror fill my ears. Were they imaginary? Or were the screams actually out in the distance, coming from my fellow test subjects in the other rooms?

I could feel myself shivering all over. No. I wasn't shivering, but convulsing. Thrashing against the hard metal table. My restraints were all that kept me from flopping off. The shadows above me – no, not shadows, but black voids within my vision – had become stretched out. Long thin necks attached to oblong heads. They stretched so far that their heads were practically touching, converging over my spasming body. They said words to each other that I only understood as blurs. Did I say blurs? I meant buzz.

One of these interdimensional beings stretched its long thin arm towards my face. There was something held within its elongated, bony fingers. I felt something cover my mouth then tasted the flow of cool, slightly medicinal air. The unnaturally shaped entities above me shrank back down into human forms. My eyes reset themselves back in place, only then realizing they had rolled back into my skull. The dark parts of my sight didn't seem nearly as dark as they did before. The faces came back into subtle distinction. Subtle, because the light behind their heads still cast shadows over their faces.

"Good call on the oxygen, Mikhail," Dr. Begum said.

"Maybe if you hadn't turned him up to three from the get-go, he wouldn't have been in such a shock," General Hawkes said snidely.

"After 36 trials we have yet to discover the key to successfully running a subject through a complete regimen. I need some kind of breakthrough, and this specimen seems very promising."

"Well, I definitely didn't think he was going to last once he started convulsing," Hawkes said. "Seems stable enough now."

"Indeed," Dr. Begum agreed, then turned to her colleague. "Shall I prepare the sedative?"

"Absolutely." Dr. Petrov wrote a few things down in his notes. "He won't be able to get rest on a setting this high this early in the trials, and we all know the body heals and adapts best during sleep."

The general left my vision while Dr. Petrov packed some of his supplies away. Dr. Begum pulled out a syringe and jabbed it into a vial, pulling the plunger back and filling the barrel with a translucent fluid. She tapped the syringe with her middle finger twice, eyeing the concoction.

Moving over to my left side, I felt the cool swob of an alcohol wipe on the inside of my elbow. I could see her place the needle into my arm but didn't feel the prick. There were too many things going in and out of my body at this point to notice any extra pressure. I watched a burst of crimson suddenly bloom in the translucent fluid as Begum drew in a slight amount of blood to ensure she had hit the vein. She slowly plunged the sedative into my bloodstream until there was nothing left in the syringe.

"Sleep well, 42," she cooed, and disappeared from my vision as well.

Her footsteps sounded distant, although distant they were not. I knew I was beginning to drift. A warmth spread throughout my body, reminiscent of drinking hot cocoa on a wintry Christmas morn. All is calm and all is bright, sunlight reflecting softly off gleaming snow that has freshly blanketed the lawn. Still so fresh, the snow could almost pass for velvety down feathers exploding out of the soft pillows you have just risen from. That wonderful scent of cinnamon and pine drifting throughout the silent home, silent world.

There arose such a clatter! The heavy metal door slammed shut and my momentary escape had itself escaped. After that loud bang I heard the metallic clunk of the lock shifting into place. My breathing slowed; all *was* calm, considering things. The big light overhead flickered for a moment, then dimmed. Were they shutting the light off? Or was the sedative forcing my eyes shut? Who was I kidding, I wanted my eyes to be shut. I felt the puffiness beneath my eyes and my eyelids carried weights. This was a terrible nightmare. If I closed my eyes, then I would wake, and all this would surely be over.

Everything was black, a dark void. I felt myself drifting into oblivion, like sinking into a cozy memory foam bed. I was laying on a feather, elegantly floating side to side as I slowly made my way down, settling ever so gently onto the ground. Stability. Finally, after a long and trying night, some stability. My eyelids fluttered as the morning light broke in.

A warmth weighed upon my chest and laid across my belly. Even more warmth pressed up against my right side. It shifted, as did I. Instinctively, I reached over to pull my sweet Leora closer to me. She kissed my chest, then kissed my chin. To feel her within my arms was to feel life itself.

"Good morning, beautiful," Leora murmured.

"Mornin', queen." I kissed the top of her head, then took in a deep breath of her hair. It smelt glorious. Not like the coconut shampoo that she used, but the scent that she made all on her own. The scent of *her*. It was and always will be my favorite scent.

"You moved around a lot last night. 'Till I snuggled up against you." Her tone was soft with concern. "Bad dream?"

"The worst! A total and absolute nightmare! But you are in my arms now and that's all that matters."

"You're sweet." She pushed herself up to look into my eyes. "If only that were true."

"What? How could you say that?"

"If I was all that mattered, then why would you want to leave me?"

"*Leave* you? Why would I *leave*!?"

"For money. Money is more important."

"Don't say that! That's just not true."

"Of course it is. If it wasn't then you would actually be here with me."

I woke up in a screaming pain. It was dark and cold. I was alone. There was something on my face. I couldn't get up, could just barely move my head at all. There was something holding the right side of my head in place with a mechanical hum. The churning sound of its gears grounded me to the present again, and that was when I noticed the blinking lights of the sinister machine I was hooked onto. It was all just a dream. Not this terror I was experiencing now, but the sweet moment with the love of my life. That was the first of countless nights I had the same recurring dream.

I was screaming when the two scientists entered my prison the next day. They were accompanied by two soldiers, different ones from before. Had I been screaming since I awoke or if I had started screaming a moment ago, I wouldn't know. I was so dissociated from time. Of course, I would come to learn how little meaning our rudimentary concept of time truly holds, but that would be later in my life.

The scientists rushed to my side while the soldiers remained by the door. Actually, I was mistaken in my delirium, they did not rush in but walked casually over. I was certain that I was screaming. Didn't that matter to them? Of course not. Had they been humanitarians, I wouldn't be strapped to this table. I was just an experiment to them. An *asset*. The forty-second one, to be precise.

Dr. Begum checked my vitals while Dr. Petrov tinkered with his machine. A warmth diffused from my left arm, spreading up my shoulder, to my heart, then throughout my body. That was when I realized that Anwara had injected me with another sedative. It felt as if a fleece blanket was gently settling over me. I was no longer screaming.

"He seems to be reacting to level three pretty strongly, Mikhail," Begum said. "They usually don't start with these mad screams until later on in the trails."

"How are his vitals?" asked Petrov.

"Heart rate is high, which is expected with the state we found him in, but aside from that, he is coping."

"Good, good. That is excellent. Have you taken note of his muscle growth?"

"It is quite a noticeable difference from yesterday, yes. The others are showing only minor physical improvements so far. Certainly not at 42's caliber, at least." They both scribbled something down.

"I think we should bring in the EEG. Let's monitor his brain activity and then I want to propose turning the machine up."

"Are you certain, Mikhail? 42 is doing well so far, I would hate to lose him."

"We drag these things out with every other patient and see what good it's done them. Perhaps the shock of intensity is what's aiding this asset here. In fact," Petrov flipped through his notes, "how about we also jump the gun and up Patient 037's dose as well? We can see if the extra jolt would benefit 37 and if not, then we still have the others on the gradual incline."

"You are the man with the vision," Anwara conceded. "How should we proceed?"

"We will turn 37 up two levels, 38 up one and maybe we leave 40 and 41 as they are for one more day, and I will turn 42 here to level five."

"Are you sure? Maybe we should just raise him one more level? We have yet to see a subject survive past five."

"Key word, Anwara, *past*. Five should do him fine. After that it will be a whole new field," Petrov said, unable to mask the tone of eager anticipation in his words.

Dr. Begum left my line of vision. I could hear her walking away and out the door. Dr. Petrov busied himself by taking a sample of my blood. A few moments later Begum returned with the short cart holding the EEG equipment. The sedative she gave me was in full effect. I was conscious, but there was very little difference between a slug and myself. I caused no trouble whatsoever while she attached the electrodes to my scalp.

Dr. Petrov and Dr. Begum eagerly watched the readings from my brain activity. They occasionally jotted notes down, silently for the most part. I could not say how long this scan took, but eventually the machine gave its final beep. Petrov gave a long whistle before finally speaking.

"This is absolutely remarkable!"

"Brilliant, Mikhail. Positively superb."

"His brain activity is like nothing I have ever seen. Not from these experiments, not even from the subjects we had in the C.C.S. that were focused on the brain treatment alone. 42 has gained access to parts of his brain no human being has ever used."

"He truly is the perfect asset." Begum thought for a moment, "Mikhail, do you still think it wise to put him onto level five?"

"Do I think it wise!?" Petrov repeated the question as if he had been insulted. "Anwara, if I had ever been curious to test the limitations one human body can take, it must be this one, he truly breaks the mold. I feel like a poor man winning his first game of poker. The rush, the excitement! I must have more."

Dr. Mikhail Petrov closed his notepad and went straight for the machine. He did not hesitate before grabbing the knob and turning it up, one, two, no, three extra notches.

"Level six, Mikhail? Are you mad!?"

"Do not question my ambitions, this is *my* experiment! You are here to assist me, not talk me down. Not to stare at me like a crazed mad scientist in a black and white science fiction film."

However, that is exactly what he was, or at least that's what I saw. As the machine churned, all color drained from my vision. It was as if someone poured water over a painting that had not yet dried. I watched as the browns, greens, reds, and yellows melted onto the floor leaving just the colorless sketches behind. Everything remained gray, white, and black.

My body jolted into the air, or as much as it could with the restraints. It was as if we were in a spaceship and the artificial gravity was switched off. My body seemed to arc up and hover slightly above my metallic table. The straps were the only thing keeping me from floating away completely.

I screamed in searing agony, or I tried to. My teeth were clenched so tightly together my pain came out more like a roar. I could feel the tendons in the back of my jaws straining with all their might, and the gut-wrenching sound of teeth grinding against one another echoing inside my own skull. I would be lucky if none cracked by the time this was through. But a perfect smile was far from my thoughts. Staying alive wasn't even my main concern. Truly, I wanted to be dead. At least then this would all be over.

I was not so lucky. If there was a God in this world, all good and merciful, then it did not exist here. Many people say Hell is a place in a pit of fire, some say Hell is Earth and the lives we live. If I had a theory of what Hell was or where it resided, then it was deep within the basement of the Pentagon in Arlington, Virginia.

The two scientists packed up their things and left. Their armed guards left with them. This time Dr. Begum did not seem to have the compassion within her to give me another sedative. Instead, all four of them left me there, arced above the table as if there were an electric current running through my body. My restraints were stretched as far as their limits would allow.

The machine hummed ferociously beside me, like a leaf blower gradually overheating. It shook, rattling on the cart that held it in place, and the noise only increased over time. I worried it would explode at any moment. I wanted to die, true, but I did not want to die from flaming shrapnel piercing my naked body. If anything were to explode, I hoped it would be my own heart.

The light above me, so close to my arched body that I could feel its heat, began to flicker in, out, in, then out completely with a click. My chest felt the cool air of the room once again. It would've been pitch-black inside my windowless dungeon had it not been for the blinking lights of that diabolical machine. They blinked so fast it almost created a strobe light effect. I was never an epileptic, but I could feel my brain churning with the rhythm of the lights.

Every tendon, ligament, and blood vessel in my neck stood out. There were veins pulsating in my arms that I never knew existed. My toes curled so tight I knew they must be stark white. Sweat beaded off my body and rolled over the sides. I heard the ringing patter of water on metal and knew I had pissed myself. It was pungent and smelt like carrots from dehydration.

Finally, the machine powered down. The surge rushing through my body evaporated and I fell back hard onto the wet table. My mouth gaped, gasping for air now that my teeth were no longer locked in place. I could feel something wet leaking from my eyes. I told myself it was tears, but I had never cried any tears that felt that thick. I panted like I had just run the Pittsburgh Marathon. Crossing over the Stanwix bridge, weaving in and out of the folks ahead of me, making it to the finish line in the heart of downtown in record time.

I wished I had finished the Pittsburgh Marathon. At least then I would be greeted with cups of cool water and a congratulating hug from Leora. Really, I just wished I was in Pittsburgh with my wife. Oh, to hear her gorgeous laughter at my silly antics. Or that hilarious grandpa voice she would do every now and then. Who knew the imitation of the way an old geezer talks could elate my heart so much.

We would sit on the couch, her cuddled snugly under my arm. The laptop would be flipped open as we laughed at Steve Carell's goofball character driving his employees bonkers. On the coffee table the remains of our dinner would be left discarded on our plates. Beside the plates would be two glasses holding a crimson liquid, cabernet sauvignon mostly. A nice quiet evening. That's what I longed for, that was all—

The Making of a Hero

A shrieking, crazed scream ripped me from my thoughts. It wasn't coming from me. My mouth was filled with the cottony sensation of spiderwebs. I wouldn't be able to so much as bark, had I wanted to. No, this was a deafening scream coming from one of the other rooms.

I tried to listen; I strained my eyes to identify the sound. Was it a man's scream or a woman's? I honestly couldn't tell. If I could at least figure out that, then I could guess who was doing it. I supposed it could be any one of us. I'm sure the others were in just as much agony as I was.

I looked in the direction of the door. I couldn't look over to my right very much anyway. A darkness black as pitch obscured the rusted metal door. It looked like a dimension to Hell. A darkness so black that it looked more like the entrance to an empty void. A tunnel that would just go on and on, instead of a simple closed door covered in shadow.

Drifting in from this tunnel was that maddening, pain-stricken scream. Soon after followed another scream, then another, and another. The wailing echoed on. It truly was a dark pathway leading into Hell.

They say the darkness can play tricks on your mind. I was engulfed by it. I was surrounded by demons. They materialized from the shadows. Dark spots from reality stretching outwards from the darkest corners. They grew spidery hands as slender arms extended from the walls, reaching in my direction. Their terrible clawed feet slid across the floor. One crawled on the ceiling on all fours.

There was a hulking presence, just behind me. I couldn't turn to see its face. It lingered there in my periphery, massive chest rising and falling with each haggard breath. Several spindly clawed hands ending in needle-like fingers closed around my legs and arms. Several more grasped at my body. The large one lowered a meaty dark hand over my face. I looked up, watching as it came closer and closer to my eyes. Everything became darker and darker still. The screams faded.

I didn't get much sleep that second night. After the Leora dream revisited me, I was mostly awake. Now, I say mostly because I can't be too certain whether the things I saw were nightmares being confused for waking life, or if I was simply hallucinating. Of course, at the time I couldn't consider either of these options. To me, everything I saw was entirely real.

The shadow creatures, the demons of the darkness, crowded my room. There were so many of them. They were faceless, featureless monstrosities, but their forms were terrifying. Some had tentacle appendages that slithered and slimed their way along the ceiling. Some had contorted bodies, walking backwards on twisted arms. I could hear their bones crunching with every unnatural turn, twist, and step they made. Others walked about the dungeon with insectoid legs and pincers, making their horrendous chittering sounds.

The demons scratched at the walls creating ear-piercing screeches. They all spoke, though whether it was to me or to each other I couldn't tell. All I could hear was the gurling and shrill sounds they made. One hulking figure had multiple arms, each corded with muscle and longer than its torso, which it used to stand upon. It swung its bulky body back and forth, ramming its small feet into the metal door with loud thuds.

There was a wailing, a moaning, and I thought it was just the creatures locked in with me. I couldn't bear it! Somehow, I was able to turn my head to the right to stare at the wall. The shadow creatures were absent with the slight blinking light of the machine.

The machine! Was that the moaning I heard? No, for I could still hear its muffled tones beneath it. As I stared, something peculiar began to occur. The wall became somewhat transparent. It was still dark, but I was sure I was looking into the next room.

I could see a figure lying on top of what seemed to be an operating table like my own. The figure shivered in place. As I continued to stare, the wall behind that one became transparent as well. Same layout, a figure on top of a table, hooked up to their own machine and the three tubes. This second figure was a little more distinctive. I could see it was a more heavyset body, had to be either Joe or Derrick. He quivered in place as well.

Now the next wall disappeared, but the room behind it was empty. No person. No table. Nothing. Who was missing, I wondered. The next wall faded away as well, and the figure on the table within that room, with its slender form and curves, could only be Simone. She snapped her head from one side to the other. I couldn't imagine how she managed to move her head in such a way when the machine had a tube attached behind her right ear.

It didn't take long for the final wall to open itself up, allowing me to peek into the last room. Here was another figure who seemed to have some bulk, again I figured it was either Derrick or Joe. This was the room the wailing came from. The man thrashed on his table, body going through violent convulsions. The table beneath him shivered in place.

The person in the room directly next to mine, either Luke or Austin, turned their head in my direction. I continued to hear that thudding sound from the bulky creature ramming its massive body into the door. The metal clanged, clanged, *clanged!* The light began to flicker above me, and the other rooms disappeared from my sight. The mildew-stained wall returned.

I turned my head around. The light had returned to full illumination and the grotesque monstrosities were gone. My room looked strange though, distorted. The walls were further apart, and the ceiling hung unnaturally low. The light above me was still at the same distance, but I swear I could have almost touched the ceiling had I not been strapped to the bed.

I could hear the metallic turns of gears as my dungeon door began to unlock. Wait, the door! The door was stretched tall, how could it be so high up when the ceiling was so low? That wasn't the only thing so strange about that door... I saw indents+ along the door just before it swung open. Was that creature real?

I didn't have much time to contemplate that possibility before I saw two oddly shaped soldiers step in, their legs long and thin. Their assault rifles lifted to their elongated faces at eye level, aimed at the ready.

"All clear!" one of them shouted.

"42 is in here," said the other. "He is just strapped to the bed screaming. Do I have the OK, Sir?"

Screaming? Was I screaming?

They slowly advanced into the strangely squashed room and as they approached their bodies shrank to adjust so they did not hit the very low ceiling.

"Yes, shut that noise up!" ordered General Hawkes who stood behind them.

The gun went off with a slight *fft*. I felt a prick on the left side of my neck. Dr. Petrov and Dr. Begum both entered the room after the general. All three of their bodies were so bizarre, so disproportionate. Begum held a syringe which she promptly capped and put down. There was a fear in their eyes that I did not understand. It did not take long for the relaxation of the tranquilizer dart to set in. The room and the soldiers readjusted back to their normal proportions like a rubber band bouncing back into place after being stretched. I remained awake.

The scientists quickly rushed to my side. The soldiers closed the door behind them, still carrying their guns at the ready, waiting to shoot, as they inspected the thick metal door. Begum checked my vitals while Petrov hurried over to attend to his machine. She took a step back. Something startled her.

"The EEG is off the charts, Mikhail," Begum awed.

"General?" called one of the soldiers, "The fuck is this?"

"Holy Christ Almighty!" Hawkes shouted as he inspected the large dents in the door. The aged military man crouched down and lifted something up. "What do you make of this?" He was holding the stand for my IV.

"Mikhail?" Begum shared a look with her peer. Not a look of understanding, but an unsettled one.

"I, uh, I do not know what to m-make of this," stammered Petrov as he lifted the IV bag from the ground beside my bed.

"Perhaps the asset threw his stand over to the door?" suggested Begum.

"What, repeatedly!?" scoffed Hawkes. "You see these dents!? That wasn't just one good hard throw. And you heard those clunks on the way over here. It was a repetitive beating."

"It's impossible. One, 42 would not be able to throw that over there with such force. And two, he couldn't have continued to pound on the door then return to the table, strapped himself back in and reconnected his tubes all within seconds of us opening the door." Petrov looked down at me, mouth gaped open. "It is an absolute impossibility."

"What should we do, Mikhail?" Begum asked. "He's stronger. That tranquilizer didn't even put him to sleep, just settled him down. He should be out cold."

"Give him half that injection," Petrov ordered, then looked me over, considering something. "Once he is out, and I mean completely out, let us unhook him."

"So soon?" Begum breathed.

"He no longer needs any more enhancements. Let 42 cool off. We will test him and see if he is ready." Petrov flipped each switch on the machine down slowly, one by one.

"Ready?" Begum was not following. Someone else was, though.

General Hawkes stepped forward and bent over me, grinning, "Ready for some field tests."

***

An empty drifting starless space. An endless void of nothingness. There was no concept of "up" or "down." There just *was*. Even with no sense of a foundation, the nauseating sensation of a deranged merry-go-round thrashed within me. *Me?* What was me?

"Patient: 042..." a disembodied voice echoed throughout the eternity of nothingness.

"42? Do you hear me?" A flash of light blinded the void for a mere second. Was this the beginning?

"42, respond." Another flash, then once again darkness returned.

Forty-two forty-two forty-two bottles of beer on the wall... what was that? A memory? The spinning gradually slowed to a stop. I found ground and I was laid upon it.

"42?" A final flash of bright white light cut through the endless space. I opened my eyes; a blinding light was shining directly into my eyes.

"He's back!" someone shouted.

"Good morning, 42." It was a kind voice from a man with a heavy accent. "Welcome back."

I looked around. I was in a white room on top of a hospital bed, dressed in a hospital gown. I could hear the steady beeping of my heart monitor.

"Here, have some water." The man handed me a small paper cup. I sat up and sipped it. My god, that water was perfectly revitalizing.

"How are we feeling, 42?" a woman asked. She stood beside the man. "You were out for quite some time.

"I, uh... I don– I don't know." I reached with my right hand for my forehead. The throbbing! But that wasn't where it originated. I ran my hand down the back of my head, over to my ear. A bandage.

"Oh no, no, no!" the man tisked. "Do not touch that, 42. You are still tender."

"42?" I closed my eyes. I couldn't think straight. It was all fuzz, like a snowy channel of static on television. One where you can sort of make out figures moving around, but nothing distinctive. "You keep saying that. Is that who I am? 42?"

"You do not remember?" the lady traded a look with the man.

"Why yes," the man said, "You are Patient: 042. Or simply just 42. I don't suppose you remember us?"

"I, uh… I…" I had to rest my head back against the pillow.

"Do not strain yourself! Anwara, get him another cup of water," the man ordered, then turned back to me. "I am Dr. Mikhail Petrov, and this is my colleague, Dr. Anwara Begum."

"Here you go." Dr. Begum handed me another little paper cup of the lifesaving liquid, her dark brown eyes creasing into a smile. "We have been taking great care of you, 42."

"Oh yes!" Dr. Petrov exclaimed. "Very good care indeed. Now tell us, what *do* you remember?"

"I… I…" I stopped to finish drinking the water, the fuzz around the edges of my vision subsiding. "I remember being in the sky. Uh… an airplane! I remember an airplane… and a military base."

"That's right, yes." Dr. Petrov scribbled something down on a notepad. "You are a fighter pilot, um, for the Marines.

You had an accident. You won't be flying anytime soon." Now they both scribbled into their notepads.

"Anything else?" Dr. Begum asked with concern.

"A dungeon... *Demons!* There were demons all around me," I said.

They traded another look before Dr. Petrov began to speak again. "I am sorry to tell you this, yes, that sounds correct. You were shot down, taken as a captive. These demons you mention, they are the terrorists you are so heroically fighting against. Envisioning them as demons is quite natural. It is just a creation from the trauma you have suffered. You suffered injuries, 42, but you are back with us again and we will guide you to your improvement."

"I-I'm not sure..." I couldn't remember anything, but this didn't seem right. I didn't remember being in a war... The war! "I remember the briefing. The briefing the general gave me..." *Gave us? Weren't there others with me?*

"What briefing was that?" Dr. Petrov's expression flickered, strangely seeming to lose its kindness for a moment.

"He mentioned a race. A race to perfect the greatest soldier. I am to become one of these."

"That is still to be seen," Dr. Begum said, "but yes, that is why you are here."

"I thought I was a fighter pilot rescued from capture?" Something wasn't adding up. The doctors traded another glance at each other.

"Yes, 42, that is correct," said Dr. Petrov. "You are a Marine. You were specially selected for some clinical trials. We have been gradually giving you medication to enhance your formidability. While you were out, fighting the good fight to protect the American citizens, you were shot down."

I mulled it over in my still slightly fuzzed up mind. "Okay... That seems right."

"We believe the serum you were taking is what allowed you to survive what should have been a fatal accident," Dr. Petrov said.

"Yes, so we are going to run some diagnostics on you and check to see how far along the process you have gone," added Dr. Begum.

"But of course, before then, relax." Petrov placed a hand on my shoulder and gently pushed me back against the bed. "Rest, drink more water. We will bring you food and then we shall see how you have improved."

"Thank you." I took another cup of water and drank it all. "I owe you guys."

I closed my eyes and relaxed, as the doctor ordered. Before I could drift off, I considered what they had told me. I was a hero! This thought made me feel good. And soon I was to become something more.

NAUGHTY LIST

Henry	Angus
Erwin	Charlie
James	Scott
Jessica	Rebecca
Valaria	Hannah
Elizabeth	Blake
Myles	Randy
	Kelly

The Night Before

'Twas a dark and stormy night,
But this one was not filled with fright.
All the children screamed with faces aglow
As the cozy town was powdered in snow.

"Oh no, not me," I said to myself,
As I count down the days from the twelfth.
I remained inside, quiet, and vigilant,
For out there are the elves, demon equivalent.

Such cheery, helpful creatures they seem to be.
With their eyes bright and smiles so trustworthy,
But I have been watching and I know something true.
If you listen to me, I will tell it to you.

They pretend to be children, here from the block,
As they infiltrate our merry little flock.
Laughing and skating so gay on the ice,
In truth they are watching who is naughty or nice.

The Night Before

They take down the names and write up their list,
It is for their lord; they wish to assist.
For he is one who should not be aggrieved
By silly children who do not believe.

No prancing reindeer could make such a sound
As the demon's cloven hooves circle around.
He'll claw into your chimney, just as you thought,
But this ancient one's gifts are filled with fraught.

A hairy black beast with birch sticks for the beatings
He gives to troublemakers just before eating.
He is no jolly bearer of fun jingling bells,
But the clatterer of chains from the depths of Hell.

Believe me or not, he'll be coming this way
Still, they all call me crazy, till this very day.
They say this is the time for love and for cheer.
But it's the naughty he'll slay, and Krampus is here!

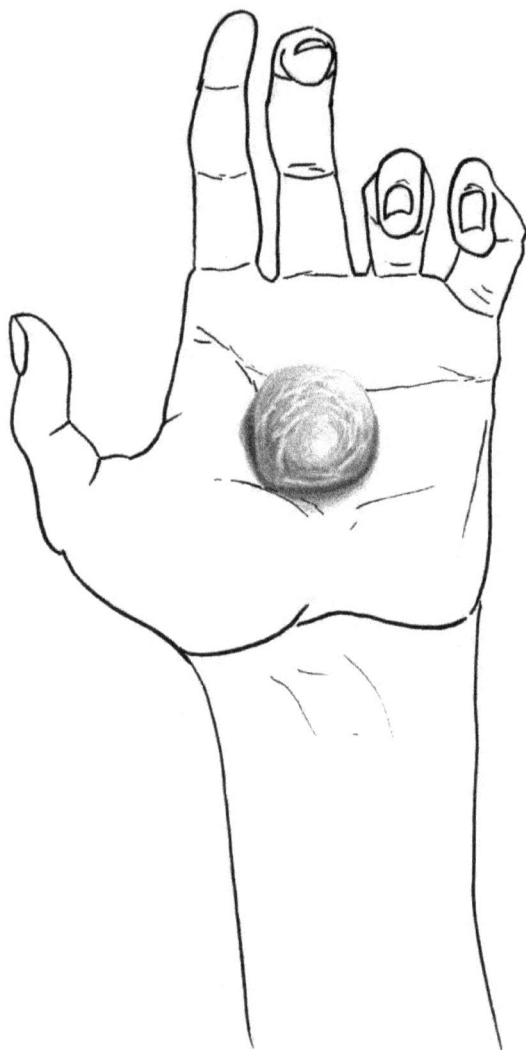

Inheritance

It was mid-afternoon with a glorious beaming sun in a clear blue sky. The golden rays illuminated the green of luscious trees flanking the long driveway. The April showers had done wonders to the yard that stretched from beneath the canopy of the trees up to the mansion which gleamed in the beautiful May sunlight.

As gorgeous as the day was, Jarek wouldn't have been able to tell anyone about it. The blinds had been pulled over the dozens of windows that would otherwise be filling the estate with natural light. Instead, there was but a faint yellowish glow that bled through the cream-colored blinds to reveal the lone occupant of this would-be home.

Jarek laid on a red and yellow paisley carpet in the center of the living room, knees bent, hands pressed against his chest. Various plates of food were scattered around him, attracting flies that buzzed lazily through the air. He clasped something in his right fist, so tightly his long yellowing fingernails caused some trickles of blood, and his other hand pressed the fist tighter to his chest. He kept his back toward the windows. Not far from where he laid his head, a luxuriously upholstered couch was angled across from a large flat TV screen on the other side of the room.

He didn't look well. In fact, Jarek's skin had a yellowish hue to his normally bronze complexion, indicating a lack of sunlight. His disheveled shaggy hair splayed out across the carpet and his usual clean-shaven face was now a full-blown beard. He hadn't washed up in a few weeks, some flies crawled across him as well, not that he paid any mind. His gaunt face held little expression and his dark eyes sat deep inside the hollow depths of their sockets as he stared forward.

His sight was on the auburn grandfather clock that stood next to the doorway into the main foyer. The front of this grandfather clock was entirely made of glass, revealing the pendulums that swung rhythmically side to side. All was quiet in the room save for the tick-tocking of the timekeeper and each minute that passed was accentuated by the audible clunk of the minute hand moving to its next placement.

Jarek thought about the first time he saw that clock and how he wished he had known then how much that classic device would change his life.

***

It had been a few months prior when a lawyer had unexpectedly contacted him. He represented David Benitez, a recently deceased estranged uncle that Jarek had never even known existed. Apparently, David had no immediate family of his own and had specifically written Jarek Benitez as the heir to his estate.

Jarek had been sent a cab late one afternoon and upon first arrival at his newly inherited mansion, Jarek took himself on a tour of the property. He stood, one foot resting on the first step, and took in the craftsmanship of the structure. He slicked his short hair back, an unconscious habit, as his mouth opened in awe.

Six wide stone steps led to a porch with white pillars supporting an awning. He could see only part of the burgundy door from where he stood, suggesting quite the spacious porch. The mansion was made of a dark gray stone. A turret on the right side of the grand structure made it look even fancier than it already was, Jarek thought.

He enjoyed the November air; it was a surprisingly mild day even with dusk approaching. Jarek decided to see the grounds of the estate before going inside. Walking around the building, Jarek came across a lush, expansive garden that started in the side yard and extended far behind the house. There were colorful varieties of flowers that had somehow survived the autumn. Curving paths of red mulch meandered through the flower beds and large bushes were trimmed to resemble various animals.

Satisfied with his new yard and having circled the house, Jarek climbed the porch steps and went inside. The door squeaked open, echoing throughout the halls like a museum after hours. A large red and silver carpet stretched out before him leading to an L-shaped staircase. By the door were two coat racks and an engraved wrought-iron bucket for umbrellas. Jarek walked forward and eyed the stairs, then looked into the doorways on either side of the foyer. He chose left.

Jarek made his way into what was clearly the dining area. An artfully crafted oak table centered the space with six chairs surrounding it, all burnished to a gleaming golden brown. A large china cabinet stood commandingly against one wall, fancy dishes on display through its glass doors. Next to it a small bureau contained the most polished silverware Jarek had ever seen. All but one pair; he assumed those were the ones his estranged uncle must have used often.

From the dining room Jarek found his way to a kitchen that any cook would die for. He paused, taking in the spotless white floors, granite countertops, and stainless-steel appliances polished to a mirror shine. On the right side of the doorway was an especially large refrigerator. Curious, Jarek opened it only to find that it, too, was spotless, and empty.

I guess no dinner tonight, Jarek thought ruefully. However, his mood quickly improved as his eyes settled on a revolving rack of wine bottles on a counter across the kitchen. His eyes gleamed as he looked over the five bottles to choose from. He quickly grabbed one at random, setting it on the island in the middle of the kitchen, then proceeded to search through the drawers around the room for a bottle opener.

Bingo! He placed the opener next to the wine then grabbed a glass from the china cabinet in the other room. Returning, he filled his glass with the deep purplish-red liquid, took a sip, and continued his tour.

Jarek wandered from room to room as he explored the first floor, sipping the delicious wine and marveling at the beautifully appointed home he now possessed. He passed by many large windows which in daylight would give a serene view of the gardens surrounding the house. By now, though, it was mostly dark and he could barely see a thing outside. The darkness pressing in gave him the unsettling feeling of being a very visible fish in a glass bowl and discouraged him from lingering too long in any one room.

Completing his circuit, he found himself in the living room. It had a large L-shaped sofa with a love seat beside it facing a big-screen television in the corner. A stone fireplace stood opposite with a leather chair positioned cozily in front of it.

Jarek sat down in this chair, savoring a deep sip of his wine, and imagined how comfortable it would be with a fire going. He sunk back into the chair but before he could even get out a sigh of relaxation, a loud *dong* shook him with a start.

The sound repeated itself, one after another. Jarek shot up and swung around to find the culprit – an old grandfather clock at the other end of the room. The dark wooden clock stood beside a doorway which led back into the foyer. Jarek approached it as the clock made its twelfth and final clang. Its face read twelve o'clock. Jarek checked the time on his phone. It was a little after seven, just as he thought. He drained his wine glass, placing it on a table on the other side of the doorway, and pondered how to change the time.

He eyed the large device up and down and watched the swinging parts behind the glass covering the front of the clock. He found a little clasp that opened the door – the tick-tocking sound became louder – and searched around the clock's face. He couldn't find any buttons to help him change the time, so he figured for something like this you just had to manually move the hands.

Jarek grabbed the hour hand and began to turn it counterclockwise. At first there was little give, but he applied a bit more force and turned the time back. The swaying pendulums made a winding down sound before stopping altogether. Once he fixed the clock to match his phone's time, he closed the glass back up and waited.

The clock was frozen and the pendulums did not stir. Jarek let out a frustrated breath and knocked on the clock face. He could hear gears winding up and the pendulums began swaying once again.

Something else happened too, though. A slot near the top of the face, just above the 12, slid open and there was something inside. Jarek opened the door again and reached for the secret item. At first contact he felt a slight shock, even though the clock was not electronic, and snatched his hand back. Jarek leaned in and, with a closer look, found a black stone. He reached for it a second time and took it out.

The stone was strange, or it felt strange, tingling his hand from an unusual chill. It was a beautiful stone, an obsidian black with red veins throughout as if it were marble. He had never seen anything like it. He raised the stone to his nose and sniffed it, not for any particular reason, and without thinking rubbed it against his smooth cheek. It felt cool in his hand, but even cooler on his face, soothing. He placed the stone on top of a table nearby. His fingers lingered on the smooth mineral before leaving it alone altogether.

Jarek looked through the doorway into the foyer and decided to go check the next level of rooms in his new house. At the top of the stairs, he found a hall with several doors and another staircase at the far end. The first door he opened revealed a cozy study, the next was a bathroom. It was at that moment Jarek realized he had yet to use a bathroom since he had ventured out to the house. So, he went in and closed the door. What he did there was his own private business.

Afterward, Jarek continued down the hall, finding small bedrooms. He assumed they had to be for guests because he couldn't imagine his uncle having such a grand home as this and still sleeping in such a comparatively small room. Completing his inspection of this floor, he was ready to go up one more flight to the third floor.

The top of these stairs led directly into the master bedroom Jarek had been expecting. The massive room seemed like it must span nearly the entire footprint of the house. Stepping into the room, at first Jarek felt as if he was in a den or a study. There was a cozy reading nook and more bookshelves lining the walls, and a set of plush lounge chairs placed near the tall windows that overlooked the gardens below.

As he moved further in, crossing the single step which elevated the sleeping area from the den, he gazed awestruck at the bed; if there was a size larger than king, this must have been it. The finely crafted oak frame was decorated with intricate floral carvings and an elegant curtain draped over the bed, supported by a carved wooden post at each corner. This was the kind of bed Jarek thought only existed in movies.

Jarek stared at the luxurious piles of pillows and cloud-like duvet covering the bed, and whether from the long drive, the outdoor air, or just being overwhelmed by everything, he suddenly felt exhausted. He let out a deep sigh and collapsed onto the bed. Sleep claimed him shortly after.

Jarek was falling, spiraling through an empty void. At first he was scared – the sensation of falling is never pleasant – but the fear did not last. Colors began to swirl around him, greens, purples, and yellows streaking by. His fear was gone and the falling stopped. No, he hadn't been falling, but suspended, flailing in this vacuum. The colors shrunk and swirled around his right pants pocket. A desire grew to reach in.

As his fingertips went into his pocket they felt a small object, smooth and cool, and he closed his hand around it. Instantly, the swirling colors exploded, filling the void, making it whole. He was overcome with euphoria. There was sky above him now, he was no longer floating in the air but stood atop a mountain. He stared in awe at the faint, blurred image of a landscape below. Jarek looked at the stone in his hand and raised it up to the clear blue sky.

The sky began to darken as heavy nimbus clouds rolled into view. The air grew cooler, though not colder than the stone he held. As Jarek tightened his grip on the stone, all light in the sky was blotted out and the ground beneath him began to quake.

The fear returned as the mountain began to crumble. The ground he was standing on lurched and started sinking. Jarek quickly backed away, nearly taken down with it. His retreat was cut short as another part behind him tore away, leaving him trapped. Jarek clutched his hand tighter around the stone. The ground below him fell away and now he was truly falling as well.

Jarek awoke drenched in sweat. His face was red where it had been pressed against the pillow. He blew out a sigh of relief. *It was just a dream,* he thought, and pushed himself up, swinging his legs to the side of the massive bed. He tried to cling to the fleeting memory of the strange dream, but it was too late. The only thing he recalled was the stone in his pocket.

Immediately Jarek reached into his pocket. His fingers touched ice and he jerked his hand back from the freezing shock. Jarek took a deep breath, then reached in again. His hand found the round piece of ice and closed around it. Taking another deep breath, he pulled it out. Jarek stared at his fist before opening his palm to reveal the black stone with red veins he'd found in the grandfather clock.

Didn't I leave that downstairs? But really, he didn't need to think about it. He knew for a fact he had left it behind before he passed out on the bed. How could it have ended up in his pocket? Jarek continued to stare at the stone as its icy chill seeped into his hand causing a numbness. The chill began to spread up his wrist and it was nearing his elbow when he cast the thing to the floor.

Swiftly, Jarek fled downstairs. This was all way too trippy for someone who'd just woken up from a strange dream. Besides, his stomach rumbled, and if there was ever a proper time to investigate a crazy rock, it certainly wasn't on an empty stomach.

Jarek turned the corner into the kitchen, then stepped back with a start. Resting on the stove between three pans, there were pancakes, bacon, and eggs over easy, exactly how he preferred them.

"H– hello?" he called out, looking around as though there could be someone standing nearby.

He knew he was alone though, he could just feel it. Where had the food come from? Did somebody come in while he was passed out and cook up some breakfast for him? Maybe, but who? There were no neighbors for miles and nobody knew about this house, other than the lawyer. Jarek ruled out sleepwalking, or in this case sleepcooking. None of this was in the refrigerator the night before. It'd been completely empty!

Jarek took a deep breath, and he shivered. Though he was feeling uneasy and helpless, it wasn't fright that made him shiver. He shivered because of the icy cold sensation he felt. A chill emanating from a solid spot within his right pants pocket. The stone.

He pulled the stone out of his pocket and held it in both hands, just staring at it. As though in a trance, Jarek slowly left the kitchen, abandoning his mysterious breakfast. He drifted past the stairs and into the living room. Here he sat down. Not on any of the couches or seats, just directly onto the hardwood floor in front of the grandfather clock.

Time had passed but the stone absorbed his undivided attention. He took short breaths, as though he were panting after a long run. Jarek hardly noticed, and he noticed his clenched jaw even less. His teeth were sealed shut and his cheekbones were rigid with tension. Tension that was also visible within his glossy bloodshot eyes. To any observer, Jarek would have appeared to be in a great deal of distress. What about Jarek?

Jarek's unblinking eyes stared into the obsidian mineral, but that was not where he was. Jarek was deep in his mind. Lost in thought. He thought about the wonderful childhood he took for granted. He was raised with love and had everything he would ever need, but as a young child he always wanted more. Jarek reminisced about his first crush in kindergarten. The two of them used to hide out during recess and respectfully kiss each other, acting like boyfriend and girlfriend. He wondered what had happened to her as the years had passed.

He thought about the good years he had with his father as a young child, before they got older and his dad eventually left the house and him behind. He thought about his mother. How wonderful and caring she was to him, and how Jarek had left her as well. He'd left the house to pursue his own life and never looked back. Not even after his mother had become terribly ill and bedridden.

The grandfather clock brought Jarek out of his trance. It struck with a resonating gong and then it struck again, and again. Jarek's head snapped back at the loud sound and he inhaled deeply as if he hadn't taken a breath in a while. *Had I been breathing?* He squeezed his eyes tightly shut and then opened them wide to clear the haze from his vision. He wiped away at the beads of sweat that had rolled down his forehead.

Gong! The clock's chime struck again and Jarek looked up at it. He gasped in disbelief when he saw both hands of the clock were resting on the 12. *Midnight? No, it couldn't be.* But the room itself was dark and he didn't need to look out the window to know it was true. He had been sitting there for an entire day. His eyes stung, his jaw ached, and his skin felt feverish. However, deep in his heart, Jarek felt a bliss like he never had before.

He looked at the stone once more and placed it back where he originally found it in the clock. With a long, exasperated sigh, Jarek walked up the flights of stairs and into his room where he crawled into bed and drifted to sleep.

The next morning Jarek woke up feeling cold. He burrowed deeper into his covers, but that did not fix the chill. Jarek peeked through his bleary eyes and saw soft orange light coming from his window. The day was just dawning, and he wanted to keep sleeping since he'd gone to bed late. He closed his eyes again for a few moments before sitting up. His mind was not silent.

Jarek grunted as he threw the covers off and got out of bed. He went downstairs to retrieve the stone. Like instant relief, he smiled as the ice-cold rock touched his hands again.

Now all was right and he went back to bed, falling to sleep almost instantly.

A few hours later, Jarek had to return to his mundane job of flipping burgers at what was once his favorite bar, though it now just gave him Hotel California vibes. While this estranged uncle had left him this magnificent home, he didn't seem to have left any money. So, Jarek was still plagued with the inconvenience of going to a job.

This time he did indeed eat breakfast. It was not the same spread as the previous morning, but instead an expertly prepared omelet with a side of thick-cut bacon. The food was still warm and there was no evidence of the previous day's meal. Maybe yesterday Jarek would have considered that his uncle perhaps still had someone on his payroll who came in to fix breakfast. Instead, he simply squeezed the grip he had around his new stone and smiled.

This new home was pretty far from the city that Jarek had lived in and he did need to find a way into town. He had no desire, or money, to call a cab to take him all the way to work, so he placed the stone into his pocket and decided to explore the garage and hope for the best.

What he found amazed him; a 1969 Shelby GT500, almost like the one in the film *Gone in 60 Seconds* with Nic Cage. Jarek had fallen in love with the car as a boy the first time he saw it in that movie. Now, mouth agape, he could hardly believe his bulging eyes. How serendipitous that this car was here. The stone pulsed inside his pocket. Just as he did with the convenient breakfast, Jarek accepted this new gift with a smile.

The car looked well-cared for, almost seemed new despite its age; he could see his reflection in the black paint as he ran a hand down the single red stripe on its hood. It was even the color he'd always fantasized. When he slid into the driver's seat, he was somehow unsurprised to find the keys were on the dash and the gas was filled to the top. Luck was finally on his side and he felt unstoppable. The drive to work was pure childhood wish-fulfillment.

When he got to work all his co-workers came up with their condolences and curiosity about this mansion he'd been given. He showed them a couple of pictures from his phone and talked about how crazy huge it was. There was little time to catch up before the lunch rush began though, so Jarek and the rest of the cooks got started on prep work as the customers rolled in.

Everything seemed fine, although Jarek compulsively placed his hand over the lump of the stone resting in his pocket. It felt like static against his leg, almost like an itch. Its coolness was comforting as he stood over the hot grill. Jarek had always appreciated the kitchen's open layout. He liked seeing the happy customers sitting at the bar enjoying the food he made for them. At the same time though, the open kitchen also exposed them to the disgruntled customers.

"This is disgusting!" He heard a woman down the bar yell at one of the servers.

Approaching, Jarek could hear his coworker was having no luck as he tried to make it right with the lady.

"What's the problem?" Jarek asked.

"This is nasty!" the lady exclaimed. "This burger is all pink inside!"

"Oh, I'm sorry, did you not want your burger cooked medium? That's how it was rung in."

"I wanted medium, I didn't want raw!"

"It isn't raw, ma'am, we cook our burgers to steak temps. Medium is pink throughout. We use high-quality beef from a local butcher, so I can assure you it's safe."

"Why are you arguing with me! Be gone, spic!" The lady outstretched a dismissive hand.

"Whoa! Hold on, you can't talk to anyone like that. You're gonna have to leave."

"I am a paying customer! Go and make me a real burger!"

Jarek's anger contorted his face. His forehead became red-hot as all the worst possible things he wanted to inflict on this person flew through his mind. His pulse spiked as the coldness in his front pocket suddenly radiated through his leg and up his spine, matching his rage. With a piercing stare he shouted, "Burn in hell!"

The angry woman fell back abruptly from her stool. The moment she hit the ground there was a crackling woosh as flames exploded around her. There was no time to utter a single word before the fire engulfed her entire body. The woman stumbled toward the door and crashed through it, her agonized screams ringing in everyone's ears as all the occupants rushed to the large front windows and stared.

The woman only made it a few steps from the door before collapsing to the ground. The stench of her seared flesh and burning hair killed the remaining customers' appetite. Without a second thought Jarek, too, rushed out of the bar. The flames on the charred carcass were already dwindling as he jumped into his car.

"Shit! Shit! Shit!" was all that came out of Jarek's mouth. *I'm so screwed*, he thought. He had just murdered someone! And in a horribly gruesome way. He couldn't believe it, it wasn't possible. Suddenly Jarek let out a sigh as the revelation struck him. He *didn't* do it, no, it was *the stone!*

He actually hadn't done a single thing – at least, nobody saw him do anything. Yes, he was arguing with that woman, and yes, he specifically had said "burn in hell," but did he touch her? No. She just fell off her seat and spontaneously combusted. That kind of thing happened to people, right? Well, whether it does or doesn't, it *did* happen to her.

Jarek was fine, there would be no trouble for him, and he felt fantastic. He couldn't put his finger on it, perhaps it was the adrenaline from watching a person burst into flames, but he felt almost high. Murder high? *No, no*, he reminded himself, *that wasn't me.*

Jarek reached into his pocket and pulled out the stone to toss it out the window, get rid of the evidence. But the moment he saw it, he couldn't help but smile. It made him feel good, very good. He gave it a kiss, then clenched it tight in his fist. Jarek couldn't imagine why the stone had made him feel uncomfortable before. It made him feel like he was more than human now. Like a king – no, more like a god.

Abruptly Jarek swerved the Shelby around, changing his destination. This stone was amazing, why was he rushing home? He needed to share this with his best friend, Alex. Jarek smacked himself upside the head. He had been so preoccupied with all the madness of getting situated in the new house that he hadn't even spoken to Alex since he left two days ago to scope out the house. *Some best friend,* he teased himself.

He had no problem getting into Alex's apartment building since they recognized him at the front. Arriving at Alex's door, Jarek banged on it frantically.

"Damn, you the cops!?" Alex laughed as he opened the door.

"I gotta share this with you, man!" Jarek's energy was high, almost frenetic. He couldn't contain himself.

"Hold on, hold on." Alex stepped back, wiping his face; he was taking a nap just moments before. "What's gotten into you? You real intense right now."

"Not intense, just excited." Jarek's eyes grew wider.

Jarek told Alex about the dead uncle and about the amazing house that was left to him. How awesome the parties would be that they could throw together. He even told him about the car and how much of a dream it was to drive.

"You did it? You got Eleanor?" Alex was now excited too and started to make for the door. "Why didn't you start with that? Let's take her out for a spin!"

"No, that's not it!" Jarek caught Alex's arm and pulled him back. "There is so much," he whispered as he took the stone from his pocket, holding it out to Alex.

"Yo... what's that?" Alex was skeptical. He eyed the thing in Jarek's hand, then looked into his eyes. "What's gotten into you, man?"

"What do you mean? Nothing's gotten into me. I'm good, well, I'm better than good. I am unstoppable." Jarek's eyes were bloodshot and crazed.

"What're you talking about?"

"This stone. It's changed my life. It can do anything I want it to do, anything *we* desire. I don't know how it works, it just does. I can't wait for you to feel what I feel."

Alex looked at the stone in his best friend's hand. Had Jarek ever steered him wrong? No, never. But what was in his palm was nothing as simple as a win-all solution. Alex could feel this, whether it was the way his friend was acting or that the stone itself didn't call to him. Either way, Alex did not like this.

"I know what this is," Alex finally said. "You gotta get rid of that thing."

"Woah, what do you mean?" Jarek's hand clenched around the stone before he was even aware of doing it, keeping a tight grip.

"This, the way you're acting. I've seen it before. We both have. You need to stop this."

"You're supposed to have my back!" Jarek said incredulously.

"I do. That thing is doing something to you. We've both seen this happen to so many of our friends, Jarek. We promised we wouldn't let it happen to us. I don't know what that thing is, but you gotta stop. Get rid of it before it's too late."

"Oh, okay, I see what's going on." Jarek began to step back towards the door.

"Don't leave yet, brother. Come on, let's talk." Alex stepped closer.

"You're jealous!" Jarek accused, fist still clutching the stone and his back to the door.

"Come on, it's okay." Alex spoke soothingly, putting a hand gently onto his friend's shoulder.

It was a mistake. Jarek reacted so fast he didn't even realize what he was doing until he saw Alex drop to the ground and his own fist stretched out before him. He'd punched him! Or was it the stone? There was no time to debate. Alex was going to take away the stone. Jarek ran out the door before Alex could get back up again.

I was gonna keep this for myself anyway. He needed to get home to focus. To focus on the stone. The stone soothed him, its smooth, solid weight. He brushed his fingers over the lump it made in his pocket, already an unconscious habit. Special. He knew it was special, even if others didn't understand. He didn't need them, he just needed the stone. He could hear it, in a way, calling his name. Calling him home. Calling louder and louder the more he hesitated, but why would he hesitate? It needed him. Isn't that what everyone wants, to be needed?

All the loss Jarek had ever faced was gone. The loss of his dream to be a biochemist, his father leaving, and the disconnection with the rest of his family. Even the memory of his fiancée leaving him for another man. He never did feel like he was enough after that. None of it mattered now. He had found the stone and it would grant his heart's desire. That was how it felt to him anyway.

When the night crept in, his mind would begin to wander down the path of what his life had become. He would hear the stone calling him until his fingers wrapped around its smooth surface. Then everything was set right, he could just feel it. He never wanted to let go of the stone again. Why should he? The stone could be his life. And it was.

***

Winter came and went and not a single person heard from Jarek since the incident. His cell phone lay silent on a chair in the master bedroom. It was once noisy with all the texts and phone calls attempting to reach him. It was only now silent because the battery had depleted itself and was never recharged. However, even if it had a charge Jarek wouldn't have heard it, though not because he was two floors away, sitting in front of the grandfather clock in the living room.

No, you couldn't even consider Jarek to be there at all. His body may have been, and the odor in the room indicated that body desperately needed a shower, or a bathroom. His face remained transfixed on the stone he held in his hands. What was left of his teeth were grinding together as beads of sweat rolled off his forehead. His knees were far beyond numb from the countless hours he had sat on the floor.

None of this mattered to Jarek – he didn't even perceive it, for within his mind he was wherever the stone took him. In his first few days bonding with the stone, Jarek remained in the past. He re-lived memories of him and Alex racing on mountain trails and causing havoc at all the parties they would go to. Through all these memories it did not once cross his mind that the last time they saw each other he had punched his best friend. He did not once think of how this man would be frantically searching for him everywhere. Jarek never did say where exactly his uncle's estate was. And that lawyer? He never mentioned a name or practice.

Occasionally, Jarek would pry his eyes off the stone to discover that a pizza or another of his favorite meals had been set before him. He became less and less interested in the food the more time he spent with the stone. Eventually the stone began guiding him towards visions of potential futures. What his life might be *if* he were to lay down the stone and walk away. A vision of him crying on the floor drowning in guilt, another of him going back to his life and repairing all the relationships he had lost, and another of him withering away into dust.

Jarek's mind grew warped and weakened. As days passed into weeks, these hallucinations faded too. In time, all Jarek could see were colors and images, nothing solid. Just strange shapes and symbols, and an eye watching him. Jarek's body laid back as his mind was everywhere else but within his vessel.

That was where Jarek remained, in his mind. His body withered, but somehow not his consciousness, if you could call this existence "consciousness." The stone occasionally continued to encourage him with food he no longer had the ability to consume. He stayed there until his body was found. Months after he was reported missing, the lawyer who had reached out to Jarek saw a missing persons flyer with the heir on it. He shed some light on the police report and gave the address of the newly inherited estate.

A whole team of emergency vehicles waited outside of the lovely home. The firefighters who broke down the front door were greeted with the scent of something rancid. Flies buzzed all around the piles of plates with maggot-covered food surrounding the petrified looking man with his precious stone clutched to his chest.

Within his consciousness, Jarek was happy. Within the physical world, an officer pried the stone out of Jarek's lifeless hand and dropped it into an evidence bag. The moment the strange mineral left the palm of the dead man, Jarek could only perceive nothingness, and nothing more.

Road Trip

Sleep is a vital point in one's daily life, providing restoration and healing for both body and mind. Occasionally, sleeping can be an odd activity, especially when accompanied by a dream. Sometimes these dreams aren't so restful, while at other times sleep seems to occur like a blackout. One moment you are laying down, the next it's a brand-new day and hours have gone by like seconds.

The most peculiar form of sleep is that which happens between the states of slumber and wakefulness. One knows that one is asleep, but still remains aware of one's surroundings. Often this can cause sleep paralysis.

This form of sleep is where little six-year-old Amanda happens to find herself currently.

Fast asleep, no dreams passing behind her fluttering eyes. She feels the vibration of the road coming through the back seat of the car, and distantly she listens to her oldest brother and her father whisper through the ether. A pothole causes the car quite the bump, and Amanda is jolted from this state into full-fledged waking life.

"Wuh– where are…?" Amanda speaks between yawns, rubbing her eyes.

"Don't worry, darling," Father replies soothingly. "Just go back to sleep. Relax."

Amanda lays back down and nuzzles her face into the crevice between the back and bottom of the seat, a thumb gently held in her mouth. Having her father and brother at the head of the car created the sanctuary Amanda needed. They always protected her. With a peaceful sigh of exquisite relaxation, Amanda feels herself begin to drift back to the wondrous realm of sleep.

Another bump in the road. This one isn't as intense, and Amanda simply opens her eyes again. She says nothing this time, just thinks how dark it seems to be getting. Amanda lifts her head and sits up to peer out the window. With her nose plastered firmly onto the glass, Amanda's eyes open wide. *Where could they be*, she wonders in astonishment.

It is the middle of the night, and it seems they are well out into the country. Now, the Emersons don't exactly live in a city, but it is not quite the suburbs either. With about an hour's drive west, the mountains come into view.

Amanda is young, but her memory is sharp enough to recall past trips her family has made out towards the mountains for apple picking, hiking, camping, or any other excuse they could find. She loves these big open roads slowly approaching the titanic forces that are the Blue Ridge. She has grown familiar with these roads by now. The sights.

They are uncovering new ground. It seems they have traveled deep into the mountains now. Amanda spots a twisting road in the distance, far below the ledge they are driving near. She has to look down and off to the side of the window to see it, for they are up on the rise. This road is quite steep.

"We're so high up!" Amanda's small voice exclaims.

"No worries, Manda!" Her brother has always called her Manda, ever since she could say her own name, because when she was smaller she would always say 'uh… Manda!' Sometimes he calls her 'Uh… Manda!' too, but she does not understand he is teasing her when he does this.

"But, but, it's a long way down!" she says.

"You got Pop behind the wheel and I'm right here," he reassures her. "Nothing's gonna happen to you while we are here."

Her brother reaches back and rubs the top of her head soothingly. There is something off, something Amanda can't quite place but still feels nonetheless. She is half asleep so everything seems off anyway, full of dreamy distortion. No bother – at her brother's comforting touch she sighs and rests back in her seat.

They have been in the car for a long time but no matter how much she has already slept, driving brings on drowsiness, especially as dark as it is this night. Her little eyelids flutter as she fights slightly against the weight of sleep. She wants to see where they are going, this is new territory after all, but what is there to worry about? She has everything she needs in the front seats of this car. Sleep claims her once more.

Amanda's eyelids flutter once again, this time on their way to opening. The hardest part of waking is accepting the fact that it's time to open those eyes and leave sleep behind.

They are no longer moving now, and Amanda is curious. What has woken her this time is the soft thud of the car doors closing. As Amanda rubs at the dreams that crusted over her eyelids, she looks outside her window.

Oh boy, are they high up now. Still on an incline – a sharp one at that. She feels a force at the front of the car and looks over that way. Her dad and brother are no longer in their seats, this she had already assumed, but now she sees them through the windshield. Both have their hands on the hood, pushing the car back.

Amanda's eyes open wide. She calls out to them, but if they can hear her, they do not show it. The weight of the car shifts back, towards the downward-sloping road. Amanda is frozen, staring at her loved ones, her family, who have always protected her. The car slowly moves backward. The two men outside lift their hands off the car. They stand in place, shrinking as they rapidly become distant in her view.

"Daddy!" Amanda screams, one final attempt to get her father's attention. Maybe they just didn't hear her before. Maybe they can still come running down to get her.

The back of the car slams into the railing, the only thing separating the road from the drop down the side of the mountain. Amanda is flung forward as the car continues rolling backwards. She screams for help, but who can help her now? She is all alone in the car and the two people she has counted on the most have left her behind. No, pushed her behind!

The only thing she can think to do is sit there and cry. She pounds her fists on the seat, racking her brain. What had she done to deserve this? She is not a bad girl, no, not usually. Had her father found the candy she'd been hiding inside her pillowcase since they last went trick-or-treating? She has outgrown her tantrums. *That's not for six-year-olds!* Amanda chokes on her tears, forcing herself to stop.

At every curve of the road the car rams violently into the railing, saving Amanda from tumbling over. However, it cannot stop the momentum the vehicle picks up the further it rolls down that long curvy road.

Amanda climbs into the driver's seat. This terrifies her even more. Now in the front, she gets a full view of the road through the windshield. The darkness of the night glares at her like ghouls from the shadows. She screams at the twisted faces taunting her outside the vehicle.

Amanda flips one of the levers near the steering wheel and the windshield wipers come on. *Wrong one!* The rapid jolting motion of the wipers adds to the panic building up inside the little girl. Her eyes began to tear up again, trying to remember what her father does when he's in the driver's seat.

Amanda hugs herself. She has no idea what else to do. She hopes again that her brother would come running down after her and save her at the last minute. Just like that one winter when she slipped on the ice and nearly fell through the thicket and into the busy freeway which ran along the back of their home. He had jumped further and grabbed her small, gloved hand just in the nick of time. Any minute now. How long can this keep going? At least the railing is there each time to keep the car from tumbling off the road.

The railing! Amanda gasps and turns to look out the back window. Does the railing run alongside the road all the way down? Amanda is paralyzed, staring out at the rapidly approaching view as the car careens towards the next curve. She tries to think back to the views she caught in between her sleeps. Had she seen this railing before? How much time would she have? This nightmare already felt like forever.

Our Happy Family

"Happy new year!" Four plastic cups of water clicked together, held aloft by three adults and a teenager.

"I can't believe it's been another year our family has been safe here," said Alaine, absently brushing her silvering hair behind her ear.

"Yup, three years ago today you all found me and took me right in," Darnell said with a warm grin.

"You mean, my dad," Lila, the teen, corrected. "When my dad found you and brought you in."

"Definitely gotta give good ol' Jim his credit where it's due," said Alaine's husband, Ernest, as he raised his cup again. "Had it not been for Jim's hospitality, our misfit family wouldn't be thriving after three whole years of this shit."

"Ernest! Language!" Alaine scolded.

"Aw hell, Alaine, these manners don't mean so much these days," said Ernest with a wry chuckle.

"They matter enough to separate us from those animals outside," she replied.

"Hey now, weren't we just toasting to Jim's hospitality?" Darnell spoke up, "Where would you be if he left behind his manners with the rest of the world? I know where I'd be – dead!"

J.A. Barrios

"You're right, you're right!" Ernest gave in. "Alaine and I didn't realize we were testing our luck in the worst way possible, taking my truck and coming to town. I know now that cities are a death trap, but we were figuring more people would mean more help."

"We weren't entirely wrong, you know," Alaine added. "Jim did help us."

"That's certainly true, but going back to the main highway since, we've seen just how much raiders stake out those areas. We're lucky Jim found us first."

"It was nice when he brought you," Lila spoke up, a hint of pain in her voice. "It'd been just us two for a while. Even used the regular calendar back then."

She paused, then hastily added, "I mean, it was still fun, just the two of us. There's nobody else I'd rather be with. It was just nice to have the company after he started exploring neighborhoods further out where it was too risky for me to go with him. I remember how freaked out I got when he went out of range that first time. But then he came back, with you two."

"We were so surprised to find a young girl all alone here when Jim brought us back, but your father is a good man. He took great care of you," Alaine reassured her. "He was so strong."

"He *is* strong," Lila corrected.

The rest of the misfit family remained silent for a few moments, awkwardly. Everyone quickly looked down, busying themselves with the food on their plates as the girl eyed each person.

Abruptly, she got up from the table.

"I'm going to go feed dad," Lila said, breaking the silence.

"You, ah, want a hand there, hon?" Ernest started to get up as well, until Alaine placed a firm hand on his arm. He sat back down.

"No thanks," Lila replied quickly.

She collected a bow that had been leaning on the edge of the table, then holstered her quiver of arrows by the doorway into the kitchen. Crossing through the kitchen, Lila opened a door and stepped down onto a landing.

To her right was the door to the backyard, locked with a deadbolt and two latch locks, one at the top and the bottom of the door. Lila's gaze lingered on the door to her left, however. This door was simply locked with a key in the doorknob. She stared at it for a few more seconds, then unlocked the right door.

Stepping outside, the young teenager blinked a few times as the bright sunny day greeted her. She breathed in deeply, the fresh air clean and sweet, then cleared her mind as she exhaled.

Lila looked around the backyard, observing the healthy collage of green and yellow grass. The garden she had spent so much time tending flourished with lush green leaves and the hint of yellow buds promising a good harvest when the weather warmed. The girl settled her eyes on the small fenced area next to the shed.

As she approached, the rabbits that were enclosed scattered to the other end of the pen. Lila smiled. She always loved seeing the bunnies hopping around, though she liked it less when it was due to fear. But their options were limited, and her dad needed meat one way or another.

She watched them a little longer, her smile wilting. Their beady eyes followed her movements as she knocked an arrow and drew back her bowstring. The rabbits began to scurry once more. Lila's aim followed as they moved. She took another deep breath and held it, remembering when her father had taught her this trick to improve her aim. She released her breath and the arrow at the same moment. The arrow cut through the air and found its target. Her dad had taught her well.

The rabbits ran in every direction, leaving behind one brown and white spotted rabbit that laid motionless, the arrow through its eye. The girl stepped over the fence towards her kill. She held the rabbit's limp body steady as she yanked out her arrow. As she did so, her father's voice echoed in her mind: *Lila, in a world like ours, you gotta retrieve your ammo whenever possible. Remember kiddo, waste nothing.*

"Sorry, buddy," Lila whispered as she lifted the little critter by its floppy ears.

Small blotches of blood left a trail in the grass as the young teen returned to the house. Upon entering, she made sure to lock the back door first before anything else. She propped her bow against the back door and left the arrows on the floor, then reached for the other door's knob. Her fingers rested on the key, not moving. Lila looked down to the creature in her hand, then back at the door, seeming to gaze past it. Her fingers betrayed a slight tremble as she finally turned the key to unlock it.

As Lila descended, she lifted a bandana up from her neck and placed it over her nose and mouth. She paused about halfway down the stairs as the smell hit her, then she continued. As she got closer to the basement the stench of rancid meat enveloped her. She tried breathing through her mouth to keep from smelling it as strongly.

In front of Lila was the third and final door of the basement. Originally it had opened into a lovely in-law suite with a comfy three-seat couch positioned across from a hefty wide-screen TV, a chest full of toys, and books collected on a shelf that ran around the whole room. She still remembered the fun nights when her friends from class would come over and play for hours, laughing over video games or making up elaborate stories with the toys.

Those evenings of silliness and laughter seemed like a lifetime ago. The smiling faces of kids her own age, the simple pleasures of snacking on junk food and dreaming about all the potential their futures held, these memories felt like they belonged to a different person.

Lila was no longer a little girl, and this room wasn't anything like she remembered it. The couch had long ago been taken upstairs for use as a blockade, and the books had become fuel for fires long since burnt out. That TV, however, was not coming up. It had been way too big and heavy to maneuver, and Lila remembered her dad saying he couldn't imagine how they had got it down there in the first place. She didn't have to open that final door to know the extravagant TV her dad had been so proud to buy for their family was now smashed to pieces on the floor. She could hear the crunching bits of glass as her dad paced around the room.

"D-dad?" Lila croaked out, swallowing past the lump in her throat. She knocked on the door timidly.

The girl could hear the slow steps approaching the door, glass crunching. The odor grew stronger the closer the steps came. Tension twanged through Lila's small frame as the sounds of movement suddenly stopped. As she slowly lifted her hand to knock once more, a loud banging on the door caused her to jump.

Lila took a step back, chiding herself for getting startled. This door was secured by a deadbolt and three chain locks Darnell had amateurly installed in a hurry.

"Dad, stop!" Lila's voice came out firm and assertive this time. The banging stopped.

"I brought you a rabbit. It's a special day today... do you know what day it is?"

Lila turned her head to the side to listen better, but all she could hear was the empty, reedy sound of air escaping from her father's mouth. She squeezed her eyes tight and swallowed down her feelings once more.

"It's been another year since you rescued Darnell," she continued. "Another year since our new family became complete. There weren't any others after Darnell." She closed her eyes as she kept rambling – the familiarity of talking to her dad again felt good, despite everything.

"I guess it's not as complete anymore, but counting the days from introducing a new member to our group is much nicer than counting the days from when we lost Isaac. And when you –"

Despite how hard Lila squeezed her eyes, a tear still managed to escape down her cheek. She hated this, this feeling of helplessness. No, she wasn't helpless. The girl looked at the rabbit again and reassured herself that she could do anything she wanted. Anything, that is, except let her father comfort her when she was feeling sad. More tears ran down.

The door rattled violently as Lila's dad banged on the other side. The smell of the fresh kill she held dangling from her grasp was driving him wild. Or perhaps he could sense his little girl was troubled. That is, if *they* could even feel empathy. Maybe not, but Lila and the others still believed that he was different. He had to be.

"Oh-okay, d-dad, I'm gu-gonna le-leave this bunny." The tears started choking her up. She gasped for strength. "You just have to step back. Step back and I'll open the door, okay?"

The banging stopped again, but was followed by a long, pained moan. Lila could hear the footsteps shuffle back a few paces. She placed the rabbit down as close to the door as possible. The young girl placed a solemn hand on the door for a few seconds and whispered, "I love you."

Lila removed the chains, one by one, then moved to the stairs. With one foot on the first step, ready to move, she reached out to the door and turned the lock.

Click!

Without a second thought, Lila bolted up the stairs. Halfway up, the basement door slammed open. She gasped and her pulse spiked. Her fear drowned out the nauseating smell that wafted from below.

Don't look back, don't look back! Lila repeated to herself as her feet pounded up the steps. Despite her mantra, from the top of the stairs, she looked.

When she saw him, it was like a punch to the gut. The man who raised her, mostly on his own after her mother had passed when she was still a toddler. The man who taught her how to survive in this not-so-new world held the rabbit and tore bloodily at its flesh.

Lila had never actually watched him eat. It was equal parts mesmerizing and horrifying. She watched as fur and sinew stretched and snapped from the carcass, gripped between molars that could be seen through the tattered skin of his left cheek. The sounds he made sickened her. His ravenous snarling and the fleshy squelching sounds of the rabbit being torn apart triggered memories of all the times she had seen one of the ghouls eating a person. She couldn't believe this time it was him. She couldn't believe how he looked.

His skull was clearly exposed in places, the white bone showing through the meaty ooze of his stinking, ragged skin. She had seen him only a few times since he'd been bitten, and each was worse than the last. There was no stopping the decay. One thing did stop, though – the sounds of his feeding.

Lila looked down as the creature that was once her father fixed its eyes on her. The skin missing from its face made this look all the more horrifying. One eye glared up at her while the other was missing the eyelid and simply looked towards her, lacking any semblance of human expression. One other thing was plain to see in this look. The look of insatiable hunger.

The young girl screamed and darted through the threshold onto the landing, slamming the door behind her, locking it immediately. Her dad's heavy footfalls pounded after her, and he was already banging on the door when the others came through the kitchen.

"Lila!?" Alaine was at the lead with her trusty barbed wire-covered bat.

"Come 'ere." Ernest pulled her away.

"H– he came at me!" Lila was sobbing now, no restraint was possible.

"Oh baby, come here." Alaine had dropped her bat and pulled Lila in for a tight hug. "I know, I know."

"Hey Jim, back up!" Darnell shouted. "You know us! You get back down now!" The banging stopped.

"It's alright guys," Ernest assured. "Let's just give him some time to get back down into his room. Let's get to the living room and get back to sharing stories. I love hearing how we all came together."

Everyone was quiet for a while as they relocated. Lila went to the couch, still sniffling in Alaine's embrace. Ernest sat in the cushy recliner next to the couch, while Darnell leaned his back on the front door.

"Jim saved my life, y'know." Darnell was the first to speak. "I mean, he has saved all our lives, but he did mine different. See, I was never much in the old world. I grew up with tight pockets and always found ways to make ends meet, no matter how terrible they may have been. My moms needed the money and never cared where it came from. So, the world goes to shit and I start doing what I do best. Cheat. I conned people to take me in and I stole their supplies while they slept. I traveled with folks, and anytime it seemed like me or them? Well, I always was fond of the idea of outrunning the next person versus outrunning those *things*."

The old couple nodded. Lila sat up and faced Darnell, glad of the distraction.

"I thought I was a loner," Darnell continued, "but really, I was just alone. Then your dad found me. I coulda starved to death. By then this world had broke me and I was ready to be a part of something. Jim an' you taught me how to take care of the vegetation. See, there I was, Darnell the ol' conman, never thinking 'bout anybody but me. Now I'm plantin' and tendin' to the crops we eat. I owe that man everything."

Lila got up from the couch and hugged Darnell, and a smile creased his rugged features. Alaine reached over to place her hand on her husband's, and the two took in the touching moment and let it warm them.

This is what it's about. This is what it had always been about. Love. Love for a friend, love for a romantic partner, love for family. This is what got people out of the worst of the worst, time and time again. Love is what brought people together to persevere through anything.

Unfortunately, not every person held love tightly in their hearts. It would be the cause of many downfalls for humanity. The lack of love was a great challenge in the past society, and now even more so. The misfit family was reminded of how loveless people can be in their current world when they heard a commotion outside.

"Hold on, guys." Ernest put a hand out to quiet them down and craned his neck around, "You hear that?"

"Sounds like something's gotten in with the chickens," said Darnell.

Suddenly they heard a loud crash. Something had broken into their shed.

"You ladies stay right here," Ernest said as he gave a nod to Darnell. "We'll be right back."

Ernest picked up a rifle he had leaning against the mantle while Darnell unholstered his pistol. Both men walked with their heads crouched down as they cut through the dining room towards the kitchen. Alaine held the girl in her arms. At first Lila was still, but then she began to resist. She wanted to join the guys.

The two men crouched lower once in the kitchen and stealthily peeked over the sink to look out the window.

BANGBANGBANG!

Both men dropped to the floor in a panic. It wasn't something that had broken into the shed and chicken coop, but some*one*, and they were shooting at the chickens.

"Boys, we gon' eat good tonight!" shouted a voice from the chicken coop. Several people were heard hollering in response.

Lila broke out of Alaine's hold when she heard the gunfire. She ran directly to the kitchen, stopping at the doorway. The teen stared at Darnell and Ernest as they sat on the tile floor with their heads so low on their necks you would think they were turtles. Lila then looked up and through the window where she could see several people dressed in hunting camo. People who could clearly see her as well.

"Get down!" shouted Ernest.

The raiders opened fire through the window as Lila fell to the floor. She so narrowly escaped she could hear the whizzing of the bullets cutting through the air above her head. After a few seconds of steady shooting, the bullets stopped coming.

"Someone's in there!" one person shouted.

"No shit!" another responded, "Y'think an empty lot would got this nice a setup?"

"Move in!" came the order, and the raiders advanced forward.

Everyone inside the house remained silent. The two men were still crouched by the window and Alaine had crawled from the living room to check on Lila. Nobody was hurt, just scared. Alaine gave the guys a thumbs up, reassuring them the girl wasn't hit. The only noises were the hollering of the intruders outside and some violent thrashing sounds coming from the basement.

Darnell looked over to Ernest, and Ernest shared the look. They both nodded and once they heard someone attempting to kick down the backdoor, they rose. Ernest fired off two shots, then sank back down. Darnell let off a few rounds before he too took cover. Bullets flew in through the window. The two guys took their turns firing before taking cover again. They hit one, then another. There were still too many raiders out there. They were really working at that door.

Darnell leaned out of the window and shot the person kicking at the door. Two others fired at him. Darnell fell back behind his cover, cursing them – a bullet had grazed his

139

shoulder. He dropped his gun and squeezed the stinging shoulder tight with his other hand.

Two more people began to kick at the door. Their efforts were matched by a similar crashing from the door across. The door leading into the basement.

"Y'alright, there?" Ernest asked before standing up to squeeze off a few more rounds.

"My arm still works," Darnell chuckled and reloaded his clip as Ernest ducked back down.

"Good." Ernest stood up and shot again, "Get the door!"

Darnell rolled to the other end of the kitchen, wincing as his wound hit the cool tile floor. Still on the ground, Darnell was just about to kick the door shut when suddenly, splinters exploded from the back door. The latch locks and the screws that had held them in place clattered onto the floor along with more slivers of wood and sawdust. A couple more thuds and the door slammed open into the wall. The guys in the kitchen immediately opened fire through the threshold.

The raiders blindly fired a few rounds from the doorway. The other two halted their fire when nobody came in through the door. There was a tense pause as everyone's ears rang with the intense exchange of fire in close quarters. Then the basement door began to splinter.

The raiders crowded around the newly opened entrance, guns raised. They waited just beyond the threshold and stared at the door in front of them, which thumped as though they were staring into the living, beating heart of the house. Ernest and Darnell remained on the floor and watched as the raiders inched their way in, guns aimed at the door. The wood cracked as debris ricocheted off the sides.

The door burst open. All guns fired. The scent of gunpowder was masked by the rancid stench of months-old carrion billowing out from the basement. The intruders were forced out of the house.

As the raiders retreated Ernest stood, pulling Darnell onto his feet by his good arm. They ran into the dining room and embraced the two ladies. Their reunion was cut short when the raiders started firing again. As everyone took cover, Lila crawled under the table and took a pistol that was taped underneath. She joined Ernest and Darnell who were crawling back to their shooting spots in the kitchen.

This time they didn't have to fire. The family was no longer under attack, although the gunfire continued outside. Screams accompanied the onslaught. Screams and snarls. Gradually, the commotion died down as there were fewer people able to cause any ruckus. Unable to wait any longer, Lila ran through the kitchen to the backyard and the others followed.

The scene that greeted her was worse than anything she had yet seen in this ruined world. Staring out into her familiar backyard, she wanted to scream. She wanted to shout from the bottom of her lungs, but all she could do was stand there. Bodies were strewn across the grass. Maybe the guys had shot a couple of them, but all were monstrously mauled. A dismembered arm flung off over there, a leg discarded here, entrails and blood everywhere smearing the previously green grass.

Lila saw it, the monster now in place of what used to be her father. It was down on all fours, hunched over a body. It could have been mistaken for someone giving mouth-to-mouth resuscitation, until it lifted its head, tugging at the flesh stretched taut between its teeth.

"NO!" Lila managed to let one word out.

Three raiders remained. Horror and panic were etched on their faces as they realized all the crew they were once a part of had so quickly been scattered across this suburban backyard. They reloaded and fired at the creature before them. It lunged at the one closest.

"Stop," Ernest pulled the young girl back. She resisted a little, then watched with the rest of them.

The two raiders kicked at her dad as it tore apart the third guy on the ground. The creature scratched and bit at the other two. The person it was on top of yelled in agony and the creature began to work on him some more. One raider raised their gun to use as a bludgeon. The monster leapt onto them from the ground before they could do anything. The final survivor began to run.

Ernest began to pull Lila back to the house; it was clear the invasion was taken care of. Alaine, upset with everything that had happened, ran back into the house. Darnell followed. The teen continued to fight against Ernest. The ghoul went for the fleeing intruder. Lila broke free from the old man's grasp.

The running man turned slightly and fired his gun three times at the creature pursuing him. His first shot missed, as did his second. The third bullet found the monster's knee. The shot did not drop it, but slowed it down. The raider discarded his gun and pulled a knife from the back of his holster.

Lila still had her pistol at the ready. The raider raised his knife, screaming in fear of the grotesque snarling thing as it closed in. Lila aimed a perfect shot right at the raider's head. Her father was nearly on him. Lila held in her breath and adjusted her aim. The terrified man held his position. Lila released her breath and pulled the trigger at the same moment. There was a loud bang and the crows above fluttered away. The bullet found its target.

"Jesus effing Christ!" shouted the raider, knife still raised.

Lila fell to her knees as she watched the decaying body of her father fall too. Clean headshot, her dad had taught her well. She stared at the body as all sound around her became white noise. Everything seemed to be out of focus. Everything except for him.

"Get down on your knees!" Ernest's stern voice snapped her back, suddenly realizing he now was aiming at the intruder.

"P-please, please don't sh-shoot me!" the raider pleaded, dropping his knife and falling onto his knees.

"No!" Lila stood and turned to look at Ernest, "put your gun down."

"What're you talkin' about?" Ernest looked at her slack-jawed.

"Don't shoot him."

"He was trying to kill us!" Ernest said in disbelief.

"We're so hungry, man, so hungry," the man said, panicked.

"What's goin' on out here?" Darnell returned, his rifle ready to shoot.

"Darnell, put your gun down." Lila only had to ask him once. She turned to the groveling punk, "How many others?"

"It's just us, I swear!" The man was crying as the lap of his pants grew darker in color. "We travel together to find food and resources."

Lila began to walk towards him when Ernest grabbed her by the arm. She shrugged him off and stepped forward.

"You're desperate?" Lila asked the man.

"Isn't everybody!?" the man's voice cracked. "We got near this house and heard the chickens, then we saw how beautiful this whole yard is."

"Thanks, I guess," said Darnell.

"You were going to kill us?" Lila looked into the man's eyes. Up close she could see he was barely a man, couldn't have been much older than her, maybe five years tops, but the stress around his eyes made him seem older.

"I don't like it, but if that's what we had to do... We're just trying to survive," he began to weep.

"What we doin' here, girl?" Ernest asked.

Alaine had come back outside, and Lila felt both her and Darnell's eyes weighing heavily as they stared at her, waiting for a response.

"My father had hope. He believed in people," Lila said, turning to look at everyone around. "You guys might not have been attacking either of us, but he put blind faith into bringing you into our home, why?"

"Helluva guy," said Darnell.

"Exactly," Ernest agreed.

"He wouldn't have wanted anyone to suffer."

"Lila," Alaine stepped in closer, "are you suggesting—"

Lila cut her off, turning to the man and offering her hand.

"My name is Lila."

The man stood up, sniffling and wiping his eyes, "I-I'm Trevor." He shook her hand.

"Let's get you some fresh clothes, Trevor," Lila suggested.

"Yea, why don't you come on in, get ya cleaned up," Darnell offered out his hand. The two went inside.

"Good ol' Jim." Ernest smiled, "He protected us before and he sure as hell protected us again."

"May I have a minute?" Lila looked up at the elders.

"Of course, hon," said Alaine, then turned to her husband, "Maybe we should clean up."

Ernest nodded and began working on the mess, piling the bodies together while Alaine brought out the wheelbarrow from the shed. Eventually Darnell and Trevor came out to join in the work. They would need to take these bodies to another neighborhood and burn them. Best way to make sure they stayed dead. The family had a lot of work cut out for them.

Everyone did their part, save for Lila. She lingered there at her father's side. The young girl didn't say much and cried less too. She'd been crying for her father for months. Watching him change and decay had not been an easy thing to endure, but she had done it. There was so much he had given to her, to all of them, and even after his infection he still continued to give.

Our Happy Family

At last Lila stood up, ready to rejoin the family her father built, that she herself had now added to.

"Finally, you can get some rest," the young woman said as she stood up and wiped the last tear that lingered on her cheek.

Final Sunrise

I make it out to the parking lot around two in the morning. There's a nice chill in the air. It's April so the temperature after sundown still bears the remnants of winter. Especially out here in the mountains. I've just spent a good couple of hours driving into the Shenandoah Valley to one of my favorite hiking spots. Old Rag Mountain. Been decades since I was last here.

It's funny how time changes everything. The lot is just a tad further up the road than the last time I came here. It is so late at night (or early in the morning) nobody is in the ranger station to take my payment for parking. I don't bother locking up – not like I'll be coming back to the car anyway – and I set off.

I'm not weighed down with a bag, nor have I brought a light. My eyesight is accustomed to the dead of night. The canopy from the trees does make it darker than I'm used to, but it still won't be an issue. All I have with me is the long black coat I wear, that I love so much. Not something I really need – the cold has not bothered me for many years, after all. I simply enjoy this coat.

The silence of the night is always so comforting to me. Especially out here where it is everything but silent. The forest speaks. You can hear its voice in the crickets' chirping, the running water of the streams, and the rustling of critters moving around in the brush. The wind blows and creates a croaking noise from two trees rubbing up against each other. This place brings back so many memories.

I remember the first time I came here. When they first opened to the public, before the Ridge trail was cut. I was just a child with my parents and brother. I was so amazed by all the green and how it shone with the beating sunlight above, illuminating the leaves. I remember the enjoyment of looking straight up and seeing the patterns of the leaves' shadows layered atop one another. My brother doing what older brothers do best and picking on me for walking too slowly. He would constantly challenge me to climb over rocks, which my mother was not thrilled about. My father, on the other hand, encouraged all our shenanigans. Oh, how I loved them so.

It would be another several years when I next returned to Old Rag. Just a few years after my father had passed. He was the first. I was well into my late teens and I had joined a group of my best friends. We had a bond so tight it did not matter that we shared not a drop of blood, we were brothers nonetheless. This time I ran confidently through the trail and climbed all over the big rocks. My friends were so encouraging and it was just so fun. I remember wondering why it had been so long since I had last gone out there, but of course back then travel wasn't as simple as it is now.

This time, I take my steps through the trail with care. My body can still withstand some more vigorous excursions, that's for sure, but this is a sight I need to enjoy. To savor every step. Ingrain each rock formation into my mind. Sights can be easy to forget. After a while I find myself coming to the first spot my friends and I would stop at. Nice large boulders that provided us a good place to sit and an even better place to climb.

I always think back to those friends, my brothers, and how supportive they always were. Even after I got sick. That's the thing with a chosen family, they seem to back you up no matter what path you must follow. Even if it doesn't seem right. I cannot blame my blood family though, my mother specifically. My illness was something nobody could understand and back then there were so many connotations with religion. As if any god had anything to do with what happened to me.

This society still doesn't understand, but in different ways now. In popular culture, my illness has been painted to be a gift. To some there is even a sexual allure, an intriguing mystique. But none of my loved ones would live to see it. No.

I lost my blood brother as a direct result of my illness. It wasn't my fault. It was new to me and there were just so many uncontrollable urges that came with it. I was so hungry. My mother found us as my brother laid lifelessly in my cold hands. She ran from me and that was the last moment I saw her. It wasn't until some years later that I watched her funeral from afar and knew that I was the last to bear my family name. I still wonder, from time to time, what she must have thought of me. Did she always believe I had murdered my brother in cold blood, or did she ever realize that the bite was against my own will?

My friends took me in. Together we learned how to deal with my illness, and the accident that happened with my brother never happened with any of them. It was simple, really. I needed to eat. From the start I could sense the almost unquenchable taste for blood that no food could satisfy. At first, I was eating rats and the neighborhood strays. Those would only tide me over for a short while and when the hunger

J.A. Barrios

would return, it was more ferocious. The hunger can only be truly sated with the blood of one species, human.

I was so grateful to have such a close bunch whose families did not mind me staying with them. I would always tell them I had already eaten, which was not entirely untrue. My brothers helped me track down prey. In those times it was much simpler for a person to go missing. I know they must have really cared for me to be snatching people for me to feed on. I know I, myself, did not enjoy these tests of will, though in time they became no test at all, merely survival. After all, the average man does not weep when he must slaughter the hog for bacon, does he?

Unfortunately, I would come to lose them as well, each finding their own end. The first, Ellison, took his own life. He didn't leave a note and we never knew why. He always seemed so happy, but I think I knew. It was because of me, and the guilt must have caught up to him. Losing Ellison was utterly devastating, and I honestly have never recovered. Not even after all this time.

Due to that grief we all shared, Vincent was the next to fall. It was the height of the opium craze, and we had known someone who grew poppies, despite the federal permit restrictions. Vincent found solace in the flower resin and we did not do much to steer him away, unfortunately. We honestly didn't know any better. Among our group, nearly all of us were chasing the dragon, though some more than others. I was just sad my condition seemed to nullify its effects. I was sad until it was too late, when we saw the craze it put our dear friend into. It almost resembled my sickness, and that is a curse I do not wish upon my greatest enemy.

Final Sunrise

My final two brothers, Paul and Alejandro, found their end one winter when they both fell gravely ill. I watched as they grew tired and weak. Modern medicine back then wasn't a fraction of what it is today, so I could do little but watch as they withered and died. Paul and Alexander each died the same way I live, in terrible pain. Oh, how I wished that I could feel that cool release from lady death myself. I had lost everyone I had loved and everyone I knew. Everyone.

I was on my own and it was for the best. It made it easier to live in the shadows, trying to deal with my sickness. I lost myself in the hunt for a time, draining blood even when I wasn't hungry. I needed the rush the blood gave. It helped me feel alive. I was lost for so many years, until I found *her.*

The hike takes me through the tall oaks and pines and the forest begins transitioning to shorter shrub-like trees. I make my way up the switchbacks and begin my favorite part, the scramble to the summit. Large boulders that seem to only barely be held in place by the precarious grip gravity still has on them. This part of the trail requires courage, it focuses the mind. Don't look down to the slight possibility of death and jump onto the rocks that lead the way up. Squeeze through the tight crevices, using both hands and feet to move forward.

I reach one point in the trail where massive stone slabs slant inward to form a narrow passage, tight enough to touch both sides without even extending your arms fully. I smile as I duck under the bolder that must have fallen centuries earlier, wedged between these two narrow walls and now suspended forever above the trail. I feel a kinship with the old bones of this ancient mountain. Further ahead, there is a nice lounging spot facing the mountains to the east. I rest here for a moment, leaning against the concave wall where my back fits in perfectly. I could stay here, it is a nice spot, but as I look over to my left, I see the highest point on the summit. Almost there.

I hop onto more rocks, making my way to the summit. Can't be more than a half hour away now, and there aren't many more obstacles in the way. As I continue on, I suddenly realize nothing seems to be higher up than the three hills in front of me. I have arrived.

Out here at the peak it is grand. The sky, such a vast blanket scattered with billions of twinkling stars. To the western side the land stretches out into plots of farmland and further than the eye can see, even ones such as mine. To the east is a wondrous display of mountain ranges holding the potential of other incredible vistas to rival this one.

I can see the rock at the highest point. I discard my coat and kick off my boots and socks along with it. I tap my feet onto the cool surface before leaping onto the rock. I take it back; this is my favorite part. Not the silence from earlier, that is not silent at all but a symphony of the wood. Up here is true silence. Just the sound of the air. I settle on the cliff's edge facing towards the east. As I sit, now at my destination, I allow my mind to sink into the past.

I recall the first time I set my eyes on *her*. Evelin. She came from Honduras. The world was changing, and America was the place to be. It had been several decades since I lost the last of my family, both blood and chosen. I had aged much, at least mentally, and I was a bitter man. I lived off the inheritance left to me by my friends, and after the War I used that money to invest in many of the wonderful new inventions that were shaping the world. New advancements in communication were popping up all around, optical fibers and the UNIVAC. I also learned of a fellow who needed funding for a silicon solar cell to capture the sun's energy. This intrigued me greatly! I became known as a promising investor and was introduced to all kinds of people seeking my financial help over the years.

After the first decade or so of this new career, I made the choice to come out to a select few of these innovative people, those I found most trustworthy. As such a respected investor, occasionally they would assist me in satisfying my cravings. One in particular had a young son who threw many lavish parties. These events in the 70s attracted all kinds of people, from the sophisticated to the riff raff. It was the latter that I always set my sights on, for those were the least likely to be missed. At my age, I had learned to become detached.

That was how I met her. She was new to the country. She had studied English in her classes back home and I had more than enough time on my hands. Spanish was one of the many languages I had learned over the years. She was introduced to me as an offering, but in that moment, as I looked into her dark eyes and kissed her bronze hand that she placed so gently into my pale one, I felt something that I hadn't in ages.

We came to know one another well. We only ever met in the evenings, I would take her to the opera or dancing at fancy parties. She knew me as an influential person, someone to be trusted, and with my knowledge of her native tongue she opened up to me.

Of course, after a while of spending so many nights out together, it became difficult to find excuses for never eating or drinking in her view. She wanted more, pressed me for intimacy. I was very hesitant but finally, one evening, I confided in her about my sickness. At first, she was terrified.

"El diablo," is what she called me, but instead of turning away to leave me to my solitude, she held me. By then she knew me and did not believe I could be a monster.

It was the first time I had ever allowed myself to love. It was glorious. I felt it repair the aching wounds of losing my loved ones in the past. It changed me. I wanted to meet more people and create bonds outside of my investments. I gained friends. I became a person again.

I take a deep breath of the cool night air, so fresh up here on the peak, and feel the breeze between my toes as it blows my hair haphazardly. I squeeze my eyes tight at these memories. Some of the stars are already fading. The moon still cuts through the darkness, but the dark isn't as deep as it was earlier.

Darkness. Just as the night always creeps in to steal the warmth of the day, darkness in my long life has always been the one thing I could count on.

Evelin and I were in love for years before I was reminded. It hit me the first time I noticed the lines forming around her eyes, reminding me of the inevitable truth. Our union was limited by the sands of time. We always loved each other but at times it was strained. I knew she was sad that more couldn't come from this. She wanted to bear my children. That's all life was about back then. You got married (whether you found real love or not), you had children, and created a legacy.

My legacy was in the two things that tormented me, an isolated creature of the night, the most: communication and solar energy. Unfortunately, I could not give my sweet Evelin children. It did not steer her away from me and I will be eternally grateful for that. Evelin was the only person I ever considered turning, although the very thought pained me that she too would have this illness. Thankfully she declined. She had already grown old when I proposed the idea and was ready to continue her life's journey as anyone else would.

All those years she loved me, however, Evelin never did warm up to my methods of sustenance. She wanted me to stop with humans; the guilt was hard on her, she was still human herself after all. I told her what had happened with my brother, but she had such belief in me that I let myself be convinced. Convinced that my heart was true and good, and that I had the will to overcome these urges of my illness, that I could sustain myself with animals instead. She believed this so strongly that I wanted to as well, I needed to.

I could usually abstain for a few days without problem, but the longer I kept from feeding the weaker I would get. We had set traps around the grounds of our estate and regularly would catch squirrels or birds or rats in them. Those were my meals. As I had said before, these creatures could only ever tide me over, and that they did, but each time the hunger resurfaced it was more terrible than before. Evelin wasn't worried that the starvation would kill me, she was confident in my immortality even when I became bedridden. It was just a spell, she said to me, and she was confident I would cross a threshold and be myself again.

Unfortunately, the hunger of my illness is nothing like going cold turkey from any other substance dependency. After a few weeks, the same game could not give me even limited satisfaction. I became hungrier and hungrier. The knot in my gut was painful, the twinge within my canines ached terribly. I remember the sound of Evelin crying outside of our room at the sight of me. Crying at the fact that this might not have been a good idea. That was my last memory before I blacked out.

I came to as though a shot of adrenaline had spiked through my heart. My eyes widened as I sucked in a deep breath of coppery air. I had strength once again. I felt phenomenal, euphoric. Then I saw her. My dear Evelin, cradled lifelessly in my arms. She was cold to the touch and white as paper. Two streaks of blood ran down the fang marks on the side of her slender neck, the last blood her body seemed to hold. I felt the warmth within my canines as her blood dripped from them onto her breasts.

I knew then the monster that I truly was, and I vowed to never love another. I never did. From that moment on I remained within my home. A grand mansion we had built just for the two of us, and the many servants that kept up my estate. I sent all the help away, pushing everyone out of my home. I was no longer going to be entertaining and no longer needed to keep up such a fancy home. I had closed my doors, my curtains, and my heart to the outside world.

Of course, one such as myself inevitably makes many alliances throughout the years to aid my illness, and those allies were hard to turn away. Someone would bring me an offering at least once a week, I never had to step foot outside of my home. I should say I was grateful that I always had a meal brought to my doorstep, but I know the gesture was more in their own interest than mine. I had wealth, after all. If it had been completely up to me, I would have died of starvation, but unfortunately it seems the illness will take on a life of its own.

Over the decades my allies, too, had aged and perished. Some had been devoted enough to give themselves to me on their deathbeds. As I watched the generations of my associates grow old, it reminded me of the pain of losing my brothers and family, and now, my love. Losing her, especially at my own hands, made seeing others die unbearable. There is no feeling like watching those you love age and die and being left wondering if your time will ever come. It is the loneliest feeling to know that you are truly alone, even on a planet with billions of other people. As time passes, so too will they, and there will be a day when I would be literally the last.

Feeling this sorrow at the passing of my allies, I realized that no matter how determined I was to close myself off, I had grown invested in their lives just as I had invested in their ideas. They were all I had now, and so I could no longer bear to see my investments age. I demanded to work with their children instead; the next generation was to inherit their companies anyway and it only made sense to pass the torch. This transition was easy, I was introduced to most of my investments' children and by the time they would come of age to take charge, we were familiar enough as it was.

Nobody ever outed me to the public, even as they introduced their families to my lifestyle. With each generation I always had a servant to aid me. A small few who were deeply into the occult even made it their mission to find more of my kind. It was sweet of them, but I had never met another. I don't even know what happened to the one who turned me. After all these ages I still seemed to be the only one. I already felt alone and so this did not matter to me. I had a roof to keep me safe and meals at my doorstep. I had peace.

Peace only lasts so long, though. I think about this as I sit here watching the black of night transition into indigo. I think about how I've watched a few ordinary people form ideas and, using the funds I provided them, I've seen their companies grow into the corporate entities that run the country these days.

I close my eyes tight and let some tears squeeze through as the wind pushes them back onto my cheeks. Suddenly a crow flies past, I hear the sound of its wings cutting through the brightening sky and nothing else. It amazes me. Its elegance is so majestic, the way it glides. Some cultures believe a crow is sent to guide lost souls to their resting place. I am more than ready for rest.

I reminisce about my long painful life one last time. I can remember all the good times fairly well. Just like the memories of all the visits I've made here. The painful memories stand out the most, though. After all this time I still miss my family, I miss my brothers, and I miss my love. These are the things one never forgets. Unfortunately, time attacks all, even with my condition. Not in a physical way, but within the mind. In the memories.

I can't tell you what my family or friends looked like. The only physical memories I have are from a photo album Evelin had made decades before. The memory of what the dead look like alters with each passing year. However, it is the loss of another faded memory that pains me the most. The memory of their laughter. There was a time I could think of how any of my loved ones laughed and it would heal me.

I have lost that too now, and that is why I sit up here and watch the horizon. Speaking of lost memories, the memory of a sunrise? I cannot fathom it. Film and photos couldn't possibly do it justice. There are some things as miraculous as a sunrise that you just cannot capture.

Final Sunrise

I take one last deep breath of this pure fresh air and open my eyes. I can see the golden glint over the horizon. The sky is now a brilliant mixture of orange and gold. I see the sliver of the peeking sun coming to say hello. Coming to say goodbye.

A tear forms from the side of my eye and rolls down my cheek as I exhale. My skin begins to fizzle. True peace is coming at last. I smile. It is the most beautiful scene of my life.

Note from the Author:
A Haunting

What does it mean to be haunted? Poltergeists in the television set? The wailing outside your window? Websters defines a haunting as "a visitation or inhabitation by a ghost," as well as "having qualities that linger in the memory."

And what do you believe about ghosts? Are they lost souls whose unfinished business keeps them from moving on? Do ghosts take control of things and fling them around in frustrated attempts to communicate with the living?

For me, these definitions of a haunting are one and the same, *inhabitation by a ghost, qualities that linger in the memory.* Ghosts are memories, at least that's what mine are. I see my ghosts every time I look in the mirror. Features of a parent long gone are still captured in the shape of my nose and the structure of my face. If I were to smile, I can see that smile I once shared with companions long lost. Fallen brothers.

My beard has grown much over the last several years as I attempt to hide the ghosts of my memory. My haunting. Those eyes, those large brown eyes that stare back at me in the mirror are the same I share with one of the living. For now. One day they, too, will belong to a ghost.

When most people think of hauntings, they imagine how they are in movies. These portrayals of demonic possessions may have some fact to them, but these are not the same as the hauntings that plague those of us touched by grief. I am haunted constantly. There isn't a day that goes by without at least one of my ghosts lurking around.

Some say a ghost is caused by a traumatic death. This I can agree with, for the ghosts who haunt me most are the ones who died tragically. I feel them when I reach a milestone, when I hear certain songs play, while I'm simply pushing my cart down the aisle of the grocery store. Sometimes just by laughing. There is no escape from the haunting.

The powers of ghosts vary. Often, they prowl in the shadows with little to no influence. Other times they gain strength enough to hold me down, rendering me completely immobile. Sometimes they grow a voice, speaking within my head, telling me all the things that once gave me joy when they were alive.

What is there to do? In stories they make a show of holding a crucifix to ward off evil or a prayer for strength from the spirits. Using a different ghost to hide from their own. I find one must embrace the haunting in order to survive. Memory is their domain, and how can you outrun yourself?

They say misery loves company, so this is my way of sharing my grief with you, sprinkled into these stories of the macabre.

So, I thank you for reading this collection. Some of these stories were difficult to write and even more so to share. If any of them spoke to you, please feel welcome to leave a review on Good Reads, Amazon, or Barnes and Noble. I always read and appreciate them. Together, we can exorcise our ghosts and lay them to rest. For it is true, the longer a ghost goes unheeded, the more they begin to twist and transform into something much more terrifying.

Acknowledgments

A tremendous thanks, first and foremost, has to go to my brother **Daniel Barrios**. We shared a room together throughout my childhood and you kept the monsters at bay… even if you did used to leave me in the scary closet alone. After a few years, when we lived in a legit haunted house, you started to show me horror films when our parents weren't around. If not for you, I wouldn't be the weirdo that I am today. Thank you for always supporting me.

Next, I must thank a very different brother of mine, **Alejandro Nuñez**. We may not share the same blood, but we share the same heart. I will always appreciate the long nights we spent in the dungeon watching horror flick after horror flick while I created my many deranged sketches. One of the shows we watched inspired "The Well," and I even wrote and drew the first version of "Stalker" (originally titled The Cabin) in that dark grungy basement. Thank you for sharing my grief and pain.

I am very grateful to **Harry Carpenter** and **Brian Hawkins**. Harry, you've been an invaluable guide in my author journey, from tips on publishing to working the convention circuit and connecting with booksellers. Brian, I really enjoyed meeting you at *The Vineyard* release and all our conversations since. Checking in on each other every now and then has been a great encouragement for me. Especially the three simple but powerful words you told me, "Iron sharpens iron." It has become my mantra as I try to replicate that motivation for fellow creatives I meet. Thank you both for your kind and motivating words.

This one goes out to **Teddy Abrams** and his piece with the Louisville Orchestra and special guest Yo-Yo Ma titled, "Mammoth." I was amazed at the technical prowess involved in crafting this performance exclusively designed for the setting of the legendary Mammoth Cave. Witnessing this multi-sensory performance became a life altering experience. I have always been a lover of mountains and caverns. I had already written the story "Death Valley" but your piece was so mind-blowing that I actually went back and changed the story to include some snippets from that profound experience. Thank you for your inspiration.

And lastly, to my small creative team of Barrios Books. **Ed**, you are a wizard with graphic design. **Jaeger**, your illustrations enhanced my sketches in ways I couldn't imagine. Thank you for sharing my passion.

Printed in the USA
CPSIA information can be obtained
at www.ICGtesting.com
CBHW032230310824
13879CB00003B/6